Christine Lee, born in 1936, was brought up in .... .ham, Buckinghamshire, and began her working life as a nurse, training at the Royal Berkshire Hospital in Reading. After bringing up her young family, Christine returned to her first love by attending St Martins School of Art, London, gaining a degree in fine arts sculpture. Now one of the country's leading figurative sculptors, she is best known for works such as the remarkable Commemorative Fountain outside the Royal Shakespeare Theatre in Stratford-upon-Avon.

Christine has always written creatively, having her first biography, *The Midwife's Sister,* published in 2015 which reached the Times' bestseller list. Christine currently lives in Devon. This is her first novel.

For my three creative children: Joanna, Louise and Daniel,
also for my ten equally creative grandchildren with love.

Christine Lee

DARE TO DANCE

AUSTIN MACAULEY PUBLISHERS™

LONDON • CAMBRIDGE • NEW YORK • SHARJAH

A CIP catalogue record for this title is available from the British Library.

ISBN 9781528988643 (Paperback)
ISBN 9781528989633 (ePub e-book)

www.austinmacauley.com

First Published (2021)
Austin Macauley Publishers Ltd
25 Canada Square
Canary Wharf
London
E14 5LQ

I'd like to thank my niece, Juliette; and my children for their continuing love and honest feedback; also, Nadine and Scott for keeping my life together.

In the beginning is the end

Chapter 1
Ivy

Her name was Ivy, but nobody had called her that for many years. Her three sons had long gone, so 'Mummy' was long gone. Her husband, whom she loved was long gone too, to Alzheimer's. He was still a physical comfort, yet he had called her Elsie and sometimes Doris. Were they his cousins or long-forgotten girlfriends? She did not know, or mind. She just liked him there.

There was a time when she was young and beautiful. There was a time when she excelled at making sponge cakes and huge pasties, which the boys loved, and their friends loved too. She and her husband drove all over the country to watch them, they excelled at anything physical, football, athletics, cricket. And she loved their picnics and holidays. She now lived in these times, such happy times.

Now, what was now? A time of struggle and courage to face the loneliness and pain of her ageing body. They had an old conservatory at the back of the house. It was old too, too hot in the summer, too cold in the winter. She could not complain, her sons sometimes phoned. They did not come down now – just too far from London. She missed the boys they had been, such lovely boys.

She lay in the hospital bed, a single hard bed that was of little comfort. She had fallen out in the night, so silly but inevitable. She had hit her head on the locker as she fell, and her front teeth were knocked out. Her beautiful gold bridge could not stand the impact, nor her left eye which was still red and swollen. She was somewhat immobilised by the operation on her hip. She turned into the pillow to comfort her poor eye. She really wanted to go home but where was he, her comfort and her joy? They said they had put him in a home. She would soon get him out.

Her thin, wispy hair stood up on end. Deep, deep lines etched her face and body, the bones seemed to stick out at all angles. But courage, courage was all. They said she could not leave, there was no one at home to look after her. They said that her husband was well and happy in the home, but she was not. She wanted him beside her, she wanted his warmth with her in their bed. She wanted to feel him there and make his favourite pasties. She could still make really special pasties and he loved them. She had not forgotten how. And sponge cakes, he really liked her chocolate ones. No one else knew how to make her pasties.

It was late at night; the nurse was concentrating on the drug round at the far end of the ward. Something made her sit up in the semi gloom. Most of the lights had been turned off at her end of the ward.

She looked about her, all she could hear were the snuffles and snores of her companions as they slept.

She saw the door with 'EXIT' written above. She had to leave, could she? Would she? Of course she would. She had been doing her exercises for more than a week. The nice girl came every day to see her making sure she was obeying. And now she could walk with just a stick, and she managed to see perfectly well with one eye. "We really do not need two," she mused.

Getting out of bed was tricky but she managed it, pulling on her old coat which she used as a dressing gown and her sensible slippers she wore to put out the bins at home. She was ready. Her pyjamas a thick winceyette she did not like at all, but she was warm. Thinking carefully and without hesitation, she looked about her. All was quiet. She filled her coat pockets with chocolate and the leftover apple on her locker. The nurses were concentrating on the medicine trolley a long way off, so she made her move quietly across the ward, stick in hand. She passed through the door. Very conveniently there were signs everywhere with no one about. A hush enveloped the hospital at night quite unlike the noise and bustle of the day. She moved through the darkened corridors without meeting anyone. How could she get past the staff she knew would be around the main entrance? All the ground floor windows were sealed. Even if they weren't, she was not yet that recovered!

Still puzzling about how she could get out, another large sign with arrows filtered through her consciousness – 'Accident and Emergency'. Of course, this was her way out. The noise as she passed through the double doors was deafening. So many people rushing about at top speed, trolleys powered by uniformed men with recumbent bodies, doctors, nurses and so many others in uniforms all looking alike. She could not tell who was who. Why did nurses not wear frilly caps anymore? And doctors not have long white coats with stethoscopes hanging around their necks? Everyone seemed to be at some sort of fancy-dress party where pyjamas were the norm. And everyone looked so ill. Quickly, she realised that she was not out of place here. She was just another insignificant old lady with a stick. She smiled and sat down on a vacant chair. Looking up she saw a young girl pushing a trolley.

"Would you like some tea dear?" she said kindly.

"How kind! Yes, I would love one, and lots of sugar, please."

People around her chatted noisily. The sweet young girl returned with her tea and she began to relax.

Someone beside her called her name. Had she been caught? She really didn't want to be caught. She looked up. It was the nice young man from the corner shop. "What are you doing here Ivy?" he asked.

"Oh, just waiting for a lift, but they seem to have forgotten me," she lied hesitantly.

"Don't you worry, I'll take you home. I had to leave my mum here and I'm just going back to the shop now."

He helped her up and took her arm guiding her through the double doors to the outside world. He sat her down on a seat outside leaving her while he collected his car.

Although it was spring, it was cold in the fresh air, but her old coat was of very good quality and kept her warm. As she waited for her new young friend, her breathing steadied; she had made it out of the hospital! The battered car drew up, the smiley young man hopped out and helped her into the front seat. She felt enormous relief as they sped through the town. She had escaped. She did not have to speak, music blared from his radio. Hip, Hop, she mused, was this hip-hop? She had related to Elvis when she was young and her mother and aunts were appalled, "Things have not changed."

At last he stopped the car outside his shop, mercifully obliterating the music. He had to go in for a few minutes to have a word with his wife. Ivy looked about her. She was only a short distance from her own home. She carefully got out of the car, collected her stick and began slowly moving down the dark side of the street. She carefully kept to the inside of the pavement hidden from view. No cars went past, not even her chauffeur of the night. She reached her house, which was completely blacked out. The houses around look ed cheerful with lights showing through curtained windows. No one saw this old lady pass.

Ivy opened the gate into her garden, walked around the side of the house to her backyard. Her dilapidated conservatory welcomed her, a backdoor key hidden over so many years in an outside pot welcomed her, and as she walked into her hallway her home welcomed her.

The house was dark. Someone had switched off the electricity, but she knew her way about. Slowly and carefully she dragged herself up to her bedroom, nibbled on a piece of chocolate found in her pocket, kicked off her slippers, let her old heavy tweed coat fall from her shoulders and somehow got into bed. Her bed with its soft pillows and saggy mattress had so much room, enough for two. She would not fall out of this bed. She sank into the blissful familiarity and slept, sleeping more deeply than she had for many, many months.

She awoke, lying back savouring the old familiar room listening to the sound of birds. Birds, and the quiet rustling of leaves was all. The sun shone through the window illuminating all her precious things, mostly old photos. She looked around. She was so blessed.

Chapter 2
The Escape

She was blessed. Her health was generally good and now the hospital had fixed her hip she could walk without too much pain. But she was hungry and wondered what there was to eat in the house. Full of happiness and enthusiasm, she carefully manoeuvred herself downstairs. There were still some eggs in the fridge and beans in her war chest. She had always had a war chest with provisions for at least a month. After all, she could remember the rationing of the last war. She would make herself lovely scotch pancakes for breakfast and keep the beans for lunch. Gratefully, she saw that her gas cooker was still working, so set about making her breakfast. And, of course, coffee, real coffee which she had not tasted for weeks. She boiled water in a saucepan, no electricity for her kettle, and put the ground coffee in another saucepan to gently roast. The coffee smelt marvellous when she poured on the boiling water. She had to wait only a little for it to infuse for her perfect breakfast. The scotch pancakes cooked on the griddle in moments. On the table, she placed butter from the fridge her favourite maple syrup and marmalade. She sat down and relished, really relished her breakfast, the breakfast she had made. It tasted so good.

The enormity of walking out of the hospital rapidly dawned upon her. They had been so good, but her nerves could not stand another moment of being a patient.

She had to let them know she was all right, they might have got in touch with her sons, which was not so good. Her sons would certainly be furious and try to take control of her life. She was not having that. While still considering what to do, she saw a policeman come through the gate and knock at her door. Would she answer it or not? She stayed very still, her heart pounding. He might be looking for her, and she did not want to be found. He walked away. She realised that she had made a decision, instinctively, almost without knowing it, that she was not going to comply with the expected behaviour of an elderly lady. She loved her sons but did not particularly like them anymore and she was certainly not going to allow them to run her life. She pulled herself upstairs, considering her options as she went.

She looked in the mirror for the first time in months or indeed years. She was slim, some would say boney, and her lined face and white chopped off hair merely showed her age. She still felt young and eager yet looked so old. She was totally shocked by this realisation. She sat on the edge of her bed looking down at her old clothes on the floor. She was silent, she could not make herself put them back on. The old acting chest was stored away at the back of a cupboard, she dragged it out. Opening it she saw an array of beautiful materials and colours. Memories of her glamorous mother came back to her. She could not resist trying them on. They fitted perfectly. They were oh so beautiful. Even the shoes fitted, with perfect soft leather and stitching. She looked in the mirror. The clothes looked amazing but the person wearing them looked old, terribly old. She sat down and wept. Very soon this passed as she remembered the hats and gloves she had left untouched. She chose three particularly beautiful hats, an emerald green silk doughnut with long snood – that would have to wait, a wonderful red felt trilby with dashing feather, and a neat navy confection which completely covered her head. She tried it on, not a whisper of white hair was showing, she dared to look in the mirror again. She was looking at her stylish glamorous mother.

Her lined face was still there looking back at her. The makeup not used for many years was still there. Could she? Of course she could. Carefully and breathlessly she covered her face with creams, applied foundation, rouge, pencils and lipstick. She was having fun. She had not had such fun for years. She returned to the mirror liking what she saw. She was never going to put on her own old clothes again. Ivy, this new glamorous Ivy she had to assimilate. 'What would the new glamorous Ivy do?' she considered at length.

She rang the hospital, leaving a message of apology for the ward sister. She rang her dentist, she could not cope without front teeth. He said he could fit her gold bridge back that afternoon as he had had a cancellation.

Then she rang her bank manager to arrange a draft and euros to collect later. It really was easy! She rang the nursing home to arrange to collect her darling husband for the weekend.

What else was there? She did not ring her sons, they could wait.

She went upstairs again, packed as many of her mother's clothes as possible into two large suitcases adding a beautiful jacket and two hats from Locks that would suit Arthur. He'd often remarked in the past that they were getting far too dreary. Now he would have a Panama and a dark-green velour with wide brim. The lightweight cashmere jacket was a beautiful dark blue. He really liked blue and would look excellent in her father's clothes, but his feet would never fit into the exquisite shoes, she had to leave those behind. Lastly, she picked up a smart lacquer cane leaving the heavy wooden stick thing she had used before behind the hall table. She smiled. She had always hated that stick. She rang the local taxi and ordered a cab for 3 o'clock, then sat down quietly to wait and consider.

She had always wanted to live in the south of France they both had, and why not? England was so cold. She picked up both their passports. The taxi driver was very kind and carried her luggage out to the car. He did not seem his usual surly self, somehow respectful for a change. Of course! It was her mother's clothes. Her mother used to say, 'fine feathers fine bird' and she was right.

At 3:15 PM, she went into the bank while the taxi waited outside. The astonished bank manager agreed to all her requests and wondered at her new elegance, wishing her good luck as she left.

The taxi driver then drove her to the dentist. Her teeth were fixed in place by 4 o'clock. It was then on to the nursing home where her lovely husband was waiting at the front with a kindly nurse who handed him over to her wishing them both a happy weekend. All was going well.

Ivy loved seeing her husband again, he was so happy and excited looking out of the windows of the taxi chatting to her as of old and covering her in little tiny kisses. Her concerns grew as she realised that she had never been to St Pancras station before, she certainly had never bought a ticket to France before.

On arriving at St Pancras station, she paid the taxi driver giving him a large tip. He picked up all her belongings leaving her with luggage and dependent husband in the centre of a very big platform heaving with people. Everyone seemed to be going somewhere. She looked about her. Where were the porters? There were none, she felt very vulnerable. Her husband was dragging on her arm, he had seen a large scruffy dog sitting on top of a sort of trolley full of cardboard boxes with a young woman in charge. He liked dogs and was not to be dissuaded. Dragging Ivy behind him he fell on top of the dog. There was instant recognition.

The dog immediately began licking him enthusiastically leaping up into his arms. Then they somehow escaped both Ivy and the young woman – Chaos! The many boxes left the trolley scattering all over the platform. The young woman chased after them with Ivy in her wake. Somehow, they managed to collect them returning them all to the trolley, but where was the dog and where was Arthur? And where were Ivy's suitcases?

The unlikely pair looked at each other aghast. What to do? They made their way to the lost property office leaving the boxes on the trolley. The lost property office was empty apart from two officials who were pouring over the contents of Ivy's cases. Ivy really did not like to see these men pouring over her mother things, her things now. She was not particularly tall but she raised herself to her full height remonstrating imperiously. She felt exactly like her mother. The uniformed men apologised profusely. Her new self was realising her power. The young woman Hellen, rather beautiful and emancipated also knew her power. Together

18

they insisted that they find Ivy's husband and an unruly scruffy dog.

One of the officials immediately put out on the tannoy a demand to look for an old man with large scruffy dog. One of the officials rushed through the crowds intent on finding them. Ivy and Hellen waited apprehensively. Where was Arthur? And where was Scruffy dog? Deeply upset, they quietly repacked Ivy's cases, leaving aside the blue cashmere jacket and George Melly hat.

The railway official found the pair quite quickly. A group of fifty or so admiring people surrounded them, all clapping and shouting for more. The old man and dog were entertaining; singing, howling and dancing together to the accompaniment of a colourful vagrant playing a mouth-organ. Arthur loved the attention and the dog loved the attention too leaping high up into the air. Nobody wanted them to stop. They were all clapping enthusiastically, then began singing 'God save the Queen'.

With great sensitivity the official persuaded the recalcitrants to stop and follow him back to the lost property office, with scruffy dog on some sort of a lead and Arthur lagging behind.

Ivy was reunited with her beloved husband, and her new friend Hellen was delighted to be reunited with her scruffy hound. There were so many hugs and licks and kisses. Both station officials with Ivy, Arthur, Hellen and Scruffy then celebrated with mugs of tea and chocolate biscuits.

The trolley and boxes were reclaimed and stacked. But what of Ivy, Arthur and her cases? What were they to do? Hellen had a ticket to Paris, but Ivy had nothing! She felt desolate. She had not really decided where they were going in France. But on hearing the word Paris she made an instant decision. They would go to Paris too. They had not been there since their honeymoon so many years before. Everyone was very helpful. They organised tickets, stowed her suitcases onto the already packed wagon with boxes and dog, also Arthur wearing his cashmere jacket and flamboyant hat. Ivy and Hellen squeezed in beside the cheerful driver happily making their way through the waving crowds towards the night train to Paris. The boxes, cases, dog, young lady and exotic couple were quickly settled into an empty compartment. It had been fun – mostly. The exotic couple were exhausted, the dog was exhausted, all three fell into a deep sleep. They awoke just before Paris. The lovely girl Hellen was sitting opposite them with a huge smile on her face. Why did they not stay with her at her aunt's house for a few days? It was very beautiful with a garden and park nearby. Her aunt lived alone and would enjoy their company.

Another instant decision was called for. The new powerful Ivy was delighted to accept the invitation.

So, Ivy and Arthur found themselves whizzing across Paris at breakneck speed with this delightful girl to an unknown destination. Paris taxi drivers appeared completely terrifying as they snaked in and out of the heavy traffic. Ivy closed her eyes, she kept them tightly closed until they stopped in a quiet leafy suburb. Arthur had loved the journey keeping up a non-stop conversation with his new friend Scruffy and as he looked out of the window he waved to the crowds as he had on his journey to London.

Hellen's aunt, Sophie, was warmly welcoming, and Ivy was extremely thankful to find herself in such a beautiful place. She could not take it all in. She felt completely exhausted after such an eventful day.

Chapter 3
Paris

Ivy awoke – the room was beautiful with high ceilings and freshly painted white walls. The heady scent of jasmine was all-embracing. She looked around, the dark oak furniture was old and very lovely. She mused: old things and old people could be very lovely. She felt lovely. The large bed she had shared with her much-loved husband was so comfortable with large, square feather pillows and fresh white bed linen. She savoured everything around her noting that the only colour in the room was a fabulous deep red silk eiderdown. On reflection she knew where she was and how she got there but had little recollection of anything else. She had been so, so tired. But now somehow renewed, she felt completely alive and awake. Through the window she could see Arthur at the far end of the garden roaring around with Scruffy dog. It was so good to see her husband laughing again.

After a leisurely soak in an enormous stone bath and washing her hair, she put on a dressing gown and made her way down to the garden below. It was magical. She stood there inhaling the smells of spring and listening to the birds, so many birds here.

Someone had loved this garden, the design, the trees, the shrubs and flowers everywhere.

This was a haven of rest. Hellen came out of the house to join her. Would she like breakfast? Arthur had had his breakfast earlier with Aunt Sophie which had proved a great success both delighting in each other's stories. They walked back into the house and kitchen. And what a kitchen! There were dried flowers in abundance hanging from the ceiling, huge glass pots of herbs and mushrooms, strings of garlic, and so many copper pots and saucepans. A large scrubbed kitchen table in the centre was laid with mouth-watering things to eat, freshly baked bread, croissants, homemade jams, butter, fruit, and lots of coffee. Ivy was overwhelmed by the beauty of it all. It felt almost too wonderful to be sitting with this charming girl sipping coffee and eating perfect croissants. Ivy felt so relaxed, more relaxed than in years.

She returned to her room to unpack and dress. She chose a soft grey skirt and cream silk blouse. Her mother really had worn beautiful things. She dressed, brushed her soft, white hair away from her face and smiled into the mirror. She liked what she saw. She liked the new Ivy.

On returning to the garden she looked for Arthur. All was quiet. She wondered down to the tree where she had last seen him. He was lying there asleep with Scruffy in his arms. They looked so innocent. She tip-toed away. A comfortable garden chair beckoned her. It was in a perfect place in dappled light beside a pond. She watched the tiny fire flies, the bees and butterflies and saw the fishes move under the water. She realised that she was completely happy.

After a while, she had no idea how long, she began to think, 'How her boys would love it here.' But this dream-like state was not to last, her boys were men now and in their forties. They were urban now, they lived in cities, had wives and children to support. They were just too busy to see them. The hospital had probably contacted them when she went missing. She knew that they would be furious.

The house phone was on a table in the hall, an upright leather chair beside it. Ivy sat down considering what to say. She had had little to do with her sons for many years. There was always an excuse when she suggested anything. They were going away on business or their wives had other plans. The world was so, so hectic now. With trepidation she picked up the phone and dialled her youngest son. He was angry, really angry. A diatribe of expletives came across the line.

"Where are you? We've been so upset. The anxiety you have caused us has been considerable."

"We are in Paris," she replied quite calmly.

"Are you crazy? You must be crazy. And where is Dad?" he asked.

"No, I am not crazy. Dad is with me and we are very happy," replied Ivy, still very calm.

"I suppose I shall have to come over and collect you."

"No, you will not, your father and I are on holiday."

"That's good. I can't get away this week," replied her son.

"We are very comfortable and have no intention of returning just yet. We both send our love, I'll phone you next week when you have more time and we are settled. You have no need to worry. Goodbye." Her son said no more.

With relief, Ivy quietly replaced the receiver.

Chapter 4
Grande Basin Pond

With Arthur still sleeping and Scruffy watching over him, Ivy could really just be. Time passed so pleasantly here. Later, Hellen and her Aunt Sophie came out to join her. Sophie, she judged, was a little younger than herself, spoke near perfect English with a gentle warmth, her friendliness all-enveloping. A huge jug of fresh orange juice and Amaretti biscuits were on a table nearby. The three ladies, Hellen, Sophie and Ivy were as old friends chatting together quietly. Time seemed to stand still.

Sophie loved having them to stay. She had been lonely since her husband died. Was it really only two years ago? He had been ill for about seven years. It all started with loss of memory. "Well, we all have senior moments don't we," she said. Then he kept asking questions, repeating them time and time again. He was so upset with himself. They went to see his physician, the diagnosis was confirmed – Alzheimer's. How shocked they both were. No cure, only creeping death. They had always been close, so together they decided to stay in the house in which they had always lived and take every day as it came. And they had many near perfect days. It was difficult for them both, but so rewarding. He still had the same humour and love of life. For them every day was a bonus.

They gardened together with him concentrating on the trees and shrubs, while Sophie worked away at her flowers. They walked along the boulevards nearby and visited friends. They played cards, Wist mostly, and they played a sort of chess and drafts. In the past he had been rather good at chess. They read books together in both French and English, he had always been an intelligent man firmly believing that if you do not use your brain you lost it, so he fought his disease all the way. With the help of friends, they kept Alzheimer's and the ramifications at bay for a very long time. He died peacefully at home with the woman he loved and his many friends who supported them both.

All was quiet as Ivy really listened to her story. She completely related to this wise and brave woman.

"It breaks my heart when I think of what I have lost. You are so fortunate that you still have your husband, every day is a bonus." They were both enduring tragic lives, but with courage, fortitude and humour carried on. They embraced without words, quietly walking into the house for lunch. Arthur arrived with Scruffy dog bounding behind. He was starving, enthusiastically eating huge amounts of the cold meats and fruit on offer.

After lunch with laughter and great enthusiasm they piled into Aunt Sophie's old Citroen. They planned to deliver Hellen's boxes of jumpers to the boutiques nearby, then walk with Scruffy in the Luxembourg Gardens.

Aunt Sophie drove her car at great speed, devilishly delighting in driving around the side streets and busy roads that she had known so well. She found the experience of driving again exhilarating. She had not taken the car out for so long. She was laughing and waving to old friends while Scruffy sat in the back with Arthur, Hellen holding on to him tightly. *Dogs are extraordinary creatures, they seem to know exactly what is going on without words,* mused Ivy. Arthur's happiness was infectious.

Without mishap, they reached the famous park on the left bank. Sophie parked and they all tumbled out heading to the apple orchards which they knew were in a quiet part of the park. Scruffy dragged them all along. It was another beautiful day with few people about so Hellen let him off the lead. He raced off; he was a country dog, but she had not considered Arthur. Arthur followed Scruffy dog in hot pursuit, racing and shouting after him as they disappeared into the distance. Ivy and Hellen were not too worried, this was not a busy London station. After much whistling and calling they eventually found them at the Grand Basin Pond where they were noisily holding forth. This lung of the Left Bank was a really wonderful place with trees planted in patterns and carefully arranged statues on pedestals. It was vast, so different from any English Park. Ivy remembered being told that Napoleon had left this vast area to the children of Paris. The children of Paris still dominated, particularly around the Grand Basin Pond.

Arthur could be seen surrounded by children happily chatting with them in his schoolboy French as they sent small wooden sailboats skimming across the water.

Scruffy could not resist the water, leaping in, scattering all the toy boats. Arthur jumped in after him, the children followed – water, water everywhere.

When the ladies arrived, they could hear the children's whoops of laughter. They could also see polite, very wet French ladies standing around somewhat shocked, soaked squealing children everywhere.

Hellen threw herself into the water to grab her dog. Sophie apologised profusely charming them all.

Ivy just listened. Everyone was speaking far too quickly for her to understand, yet they all became the best of friends promising to meet the following day.

Still very wet they found some chairs and sat in the sun to dry off. They all agreed that it was a delightful way to spend an afternoon. Eventually, tired and happy they made their way back to the car with Sophie driving home a little less enthusiastically.

After so much excitement, Ivy took Arthur by the hand leading him up to their splendid bedroom where they instantly fell asleep.

Over dinner with more delicious food and wine, the four hardly noticed the evening shadows drawing in so comfortable where they in each other's company. At last Ivy spoke. "Darling Hellen, we know so much yet so little about you. Do tell us your story."

All was quiet, the sorties of the day before forgotten.

"I was beautiful, even as a child people remarked on my beauty, yet I hardly noticed. I preferred to be outside with the animals I loved. I grew up in a matriarchal household, no brothers or father around so knew little of men's characters and very different ways of thinking and doing. For a long time, I wanted to be a vet."

"What a waste, you are so beautiful, you must go to London and become a top model."

"There was no denying my mother, so I signed up with a top model agency and became successful."

"Were you not happy?" queried Ivy. Hellen hesitated.

"Sometimes yes, sometimes no," she answered.

"I missed the country terribly, I found the frenzy of the modelling world completely exhausting and unreal, so I married a rich man from the city." she whispered.

"Did I love him? I'm not sure. Everyone around me thought we were a good match. After all, he was tall good-looking and very well connected. I was beautiful." She paused. "Anyway, I grew to love him, trusting him completely."

In the silence that followed Ivy wondered what had happened, and why this beautiful girl seemed so sad and alone.

"The travelling, friends and parties were wonderful. The white stucco house in Chelsea was wonderful. He was pretty wonderful. All seemed too perfect for I don't know how many years."

Hellen found it almost impossible to carry on, overwhelmed with emotion.

"Anyway, the bubble burst when I found out that he was sleeping with one of my best friends. The pain was incredible. Many long months of indescribable pain. He said he loved me, he just wanted us both. What was I to do? I thought long and hard. It was not easy. In the end I took a deep breath, taking my courage in both hands I left. I had no plans and nowhere to go. Do you know he really could not understand why?"

All was quiet. Aunt Sophie bustled about making coffee. Ivy sat still, feeling the girl's pain. Arthur disappeared into the garden with Scruffy.

Hellen resumed, "I did not know what to do. I did not want to admit to my mother the breakdown of my very successful marriage, so I hopped on a plane to Paris arriving here about two years ago. Aunt Sophie was on her own. She asked no questions, and the healing began, and there were very deep wounds."

"In time I returned home to Devon, rented a tiny cottage and began designing jumpers. I thought they were so off-beat that nobody would want them, certainly not in Devon, so I thought I would try them out on my aunt in Paris. Aunt Sophie loved them, also the boutiques nearby loved them. Now I have a small business bringing my designs over twice a year."

The coffee was excellent, the bond between the niece and her aunt was tangible.

Chapter 5
Shopping a la Francaise

The next day over breakfast, another delicious breakfast, Hellen and Ivy discussed plans for the day. Hellen thought it would be a good idea for Ivy to buy some more comfortable clothes; perhaps some casual trousers and a blazer. Ivy agreed, all her mother's clothes were incredibly smart. She certainly felt a little out of her depth at times. Hellen knew all the good boutiques in the area and it did not take long for Ivy to become acclimatised to this very intimate way of shopping. Here in Paris it was very different from the hustle and bustle of an English department store. The mature assistant in charge was charming, really concentrating on Ivy and her needs. Ivy was enjoying herself enormously. In the past it had always been a dash into some store or other finding clothes by herself, then taking them through crowds of people to a communal changing room. She hated communal changing rooms and the off-hand girls policing the clothes.

"Wait here, only five garments," they would shout.

So many rules! There were so many rules in England now. France seemed different, most people ignoring any rules, anyway this part of France was different. She ended up buying the most beautiful trousers which were so comfortable, and a blazer too. It was a perfect fit in a lovely colour. She thought it crimson, in such soft material. Ivy was mesmerised. To finish it off, the manageress threw in a soft silky blouse which she had loved and a cotton T-shirt. They were all delighted with her purchases. Ivy, Hellen and the manageress ended up sitting together eating fondants and drinking coffee.

"You look so beautiful in my clothes, you have such a perfect figure," the manageress repeated.

29

Ivy had not been complimented for many years, and the lovely lady in the boutique had said it more than once. Ivy could see that she meant it. Hellen was delighted too.

"You do look so good, and years younger. In fact, you look wonderful. Let me do your hair when we get back."

Ivy smiled. She could not stop smiling.

Arthur had been shopping too with Sophie. On returning to the house Ivy threw her arms around her rather shabby husband, noting his new Parisian haircut.

"I do so love you Arthur, but what has happened to your hair? Your beautiful long hair is gone! I suppose it will grow again. A really short cut is not really you."

Arthur grinned, he liked his new haircut, he also liked this new Ivy, or was it Margaret or Diana? He couldn't remember.

Ivy pulled out the George Melly hat, giving it to her hirsute husband. He looked at it with undisguised pleasure, immediately putting it on. His persona changed with the hat. He wanted to go out for a drive with Sophie, to show it off. So, in Sophie's old Citroen they left.

They loved driving together, Arthur waving, raising his hat to every pretty lady he saw. "Hello, gorgeous," he called out to one grumpy old lady with an umbrella.

"Don't be so rude!" she spat back at him. He was surprised, he only wanted to be friendly. He decided to try again, this time he shouted to a jeans-and-braces young man on a bike, his long fair hair flying behind.

"You need a haircut!" he shouted cheerily.

"Give me your hat Grandpa, and I'll get it done," he jovially replied.

Arthur loved his new hat and clung on to it. The world loved this new Arthur in his new hat, laughing and cheering him along the way.

Ivy stayed at home with Hellen that afternoon, allowing her to re-shape her rather wispy hair. She watched, fascinating as Hellen carefully brushed, combed and re-styled. At last, sitting back she looked in the mirror; a smart haircut had made such a difference. Ivy was now looking at an elegant confident lady, and she liked her.

Arthur had had such a wonderful time with Sophie, they had made so many new friends that he arrived back home exhausted. He and Scruffy crept to their favourite spot at the bottom of the garden. Sophie loved Ivy's new haircut. She loved Arthur's too – very a la mode. She had not had so much fun for ages. They had even been invited out to supper with an old friend she had not seen in years.

The ladies retired to their beds for a well-needed siesta. Sometime later, Ivy was woken by Arthur and a huge shaggy dog jumping all over her enthusiastically licking her face.

Apparently, it was time for tea in the garden before going out for the evening. Ivy had not been out in the evening for years, she felt somewhat nervous. She bathed at length, then looking into the wardrobe at her mother's clothes she quickly chose a blue summer dress with huge cream bow at the neck. She put it on. It almost took her breath away when she saw her reflection in the mirror. The new Ivy looked really rather beautiful. Confidence was all when meeting new people, she thought.

The evening was a great success. Sophie was obviously delighted to be renewing old friendships. Her husband's great friend Claud was delighted with her.

"But you look so young, and still so beautiful," he kept repeating first in French then in English.

Hellen was also delighted with Didier, his son, who was charming and obviously intrigued by her.

"Tell me more about yourself. How is it for you in Devon?" he kept asking.

Hellen just smiled. As yet she did not want flirting. Ivy and Arthur were entertained by the two elderly aunts and a talking parrot.

All this, as they consumed delicious food and imbibed exquisite wine. Ivy had not tasted wine like this for many, many years, if ever! It had been a good day.

The following day, a Friday, Ivy decided to try phoning her son again. He had probably got over his initial anger. He would surely be more civilised. She sat again in the big leather armchair and dialled his number.

"Hello darling, how are you?" she ventured.

"Thank you for calling, Mother, I'm well, I have taken the week off and am catching the next plane to Paris," he replied.

"Really, how nice and when will you arrive?" she said hesitantly.

"About 4 PM, give me your address."

Giving him her address, the phone call ended. "Goodbye," replied Ivy speaking into the leather armchair.

Ivy had to absorb the fact that her son was coming over to confront her, expecting to take them back home. She did not want this at all and considered what to do.

Ivy had not been a particularly religious person, but as she sat there alone, she felt a real need for a father figure, she needed advice. Her father had been gone long ago, she still looked for a strength greater than hers, not just in dealing with her son but also dealing with herself. The future of coping with Arthur and Alzheimer's would be a trial. She knew the disease was progressive. She also knew she needed support, a great deal of support. She decided to go to the Notre Dame Cathedral. She remembered going there on her honeymoon with Arthur, remembering the tremendous spirituality which surrounded them there. Hellen and Sophie were happy to have Arthur and Scruffy for the day, making plans to go to the park again before then going on to the Eiffel tower.

Chapter 6
The Notre Dame Cathedral

Ivy took a bus into the centre of Paris which went past the Louvre museum that she remembered well. It had all been so elegant then. Now there were so many buses clogging up the streets and so many people on the pavements, not at all as she remembered it. Her bus slowly ploughed on with more and more people blocking the road. She could scarcely believe it. The tranquil place of her memory was now a sea of activity and noise. At last she arrived at the Notre Dame. Who could not be impressed by this huge magnificent building? Yet, she was nearly knocked down by the sheer volume of human traffic. There were long, long queues of people waiting to get into the inner sanctum of the Cathedral. Numbers of police encased in heavy black uniforms carrying enormous intimidating guns watched over them. Somewhat shocked and horrified, Ivy joined one of the queues and waited. She felt uncomfortable. Fearful of the pushing noisy crowds, all shouting in so many different languages. Thankfully after an hour's waiting, she moved into the Cathedral. There were as many people inside as out. What could she do? She felt overwhelmed, she came here for peace and spirituality. There was none. She saw a sign, discretely displayed 'Mass 12.30'.

It had to be better than being forced along by the crowds. She crept into the cordoned off area and waited. A few people joined her. Minutes later a hush seemed to envelop the entire building. Three priests in heavily embroidered vestments quietly entered the sacristy making their way towards the altar. They began the Mass, in French of course. Ivy was able to follow some of it which was reassuring, but in the roped off area with less than 30 other people she realised that they were all part of a floor show which the thousands who were flocking around had come to see. She did not like it. She felt like a fish in a goldfish bowl. Nevertheless, she stayed until the end. Quietly leaving she followed the priests to their sanctuary behind a heavy door that they firmly closed behind them. Ivy continued down a side isle and found herself alone in the Sacrarium. She was by herself and could look around at all the treasures quietly. The paintings of past Popes dominated along the walls. Exquisite pieces of gold and silver rested on shelves, and there were relics, dubious relics which she could not appreciate, but she felt at peace alone in this place. She was aware of a higher power waiting to help her.

Making her way back through the throng of people to the outside she saw that there were still hundreds of people in queues and still so many police in black combat uniforms carrying those big intimidating guns. Exhausted, Ivy struggled over a bridge nearby to get away from it all. She actually found a tea shop.

This English tea shop had pretty tablecloths and a very young girl in charge. It was empty.

This oasis in the heart of Paris was her oasis. She sat down, ordered a pot of Earl Grey tea and a chocolate brownie. It felt a bit like home. Ivy began to relax drinking the familiar Earl Grey and nibbling the chocolate brownie. She took out her diary still in her bag untouched for many days, and began to write.

In time, she became aware of a tall young man bending over her. He began to speak in heavily accented French. "*Non. Doucement, je parle seulment un tres petit francais,*" she stammered. The young man stared at her for a long time.

"You so beautiful," he said quietly.

"Me. Oh, no, no," Ivy replied aghast. He pointed to her diary.

"And such beautiful writing," he said shaking his head. "Where you live?"

Ivy, ever open and generous, gave him Sophie's address. He left her smiling, "*Merci, merci,* I vil visit soon." Thoughts ran through Ivy's head. She did not know this charming man and rather hoped he would not visit. She had never been picked up in a tea shop before, and certainly not a good-looking young man with black beard and little English.

After a while Ivy left the teashop. She wanted to find the ancient church which was advertising a concert of piano music nearby.

She knew Sophie would enjoy it and she wanted to do something for her. The church, Eglise Saint Julien le Pauvre, she could not find. A visiting Chinese couple, who spoke perfect English, appeared from nowhere. They knew where it was almost hidden from view but, there was nowhere to buy tickets. Ivy understood that she had to buy tickets for the event half an hour before the performance. She lingered in this tiny church, a real sanctuary, yet only a few hundred yards from the milling noisy people clamouring to get into the Notre Dame. This, the oldest church in Paris, was a real place of peace. Ivy knelt down and prayed, really prayed, for the first time in many years.

Later, much later after getting lost, with sore feet and aching back she arrived back at Sophie's house. They were all bubbling with excitement. The park had been great fun and the Eiffel tower quite an experience, apart from Arthur trying to sit on a top ledge shouting that he was a bird and was going to fly. It had been really worrying at the time but was now forgotten in the retelling over a delicious glass of cold white wine sitting in the garden.

They all thought that the concert was a great idea. At 7 o'clock, they left for the old church of Saint Julien le Pauvre. A Steinway grand piano had been imported into the front. Incredible! How did they do it? There was going to be a recital of Chopin, by Herbert du Plessis. Arthur was excited as ever by anything new, firmly marching through the seating to the front row. It was a beautiful evening, the music an absolute delight although Arthur decided to join another party nearby with a small boy, who kept making faces. Nobody seemed to mind, the music overwhelming any other consideration.

The next day was taken up with general activities around the house in preparation for Ivy's son, Edward. Then it was a trip to the market. What a market! Everyone was shouting and laughing, haggling over prices and pinching the flesh of peaches and small children. There were enormous fleshy yellow pears, large purple things that Ivy had never seen in England. Watermelons lay in great heaps on the ground and so many exotic vegetables. It was breathtaking. Ivy was used to organised English supermarkets. There were butchers with meat hung and cut in extraordinary ways. There were wonderful fish, some huge with vicious jaws, and crabs, and prawns and lobsters still alive! Hanging bunches of sweet-smelling herbs vied with plaited garlic and huge onions hung in long swathes from the handlebars of ancient bicycles. And such enormous tomatoes!

Back home in Sophie's garden, a rather exhausted Ivy made her way to her favourite seat where she promptly dozed off while Sophie and Hellen went to unpack in the kitchen. All was quiet.

Edward arrived through the garden gate, so was able to absorb this peaceful scene hidden away from the noise and bustle of central Paris. Could his mother really be here? Scruffy was the first to greet him, almost knocking him over and licking him passionately. This was followed by his father who was equally demonstrative, vying with Scruffy for attention. Laughing, he dragged his case towards the house. He saw Ivy, his mother, asleep on the garden seat. He stopped to look at her, she looked different somehow. A sort of beauty had enveloped her, and as he bent over to kiss her, she opened her eyes.

The moment she had dreaded wasn't there after all. Her son was there for her smiling, and with love in his eyes.

Chapter 7
Edward

Edward embraced his mother. He could not remember doing that spontaneously for many years. She had always looked so needy, but this Ivy, his mother, was different, smelling of lavender and wild garlic. This Ivy seemed rejuvenated. Happily, they walked together into the house. He noticed that she no longer limped or looked in pain.

"The hospital has done a good job," he remarked.

"Yes, they have, and I am very grateful. Do meet our new friends, Hellen and Sophie."

What a fabulous girl, thought Edward, as he gazed at Hellen in wonder.

They chatted about his journey, how much they loved his parents insisting that he stay with them. Their relaxed generosity amazed this rather stiff English man in a pinstriped suit. Later, when Arthur joined them, the conversation deteriorated into wonderful childish fun. Was this happy man his father?

When alone together, Ivy and Edward were able to catch up, not only the past few weeks but also years. Edward spoke:

"I'm here because I've been made redundant, and Valerie has left me. I thought I would check up on you and Dad."

Ivy could see the real pain in her son's eyes and loved him the more for it.

"I am sorry, really sorry, I have given you such a shock discharging myself from the hospital and leaving as I did. I just could not stand being a patient for another minute. And I missed your father dreadfully. I had not worked it out beforehand, it was a spur of the moment decision but as you can see it has all worked out amazingly. Your father and I are so very happy. How long it will last I don't know, but we are living for the moment, leaving the future to look after itself."

As Edward listened to his mother, his heart went out to this brave little woman.

"I do understand. It cannot have been easy. It is so good to see you both so well. I would like to help as much as I can. After all I have no job now, and no one else in the world to care for – or who cares for me," he added.

Ivy was so touched by his words. Was this really her preoccupied son of yesteryear? She took him into her arms and hugged him.

"It is so very good to see you. I no longer have a limp now as most of my pain has gone. I am no longer a burden to anyone. I had not realised that my hip had got so bad. The hospital certainly sorted it out and although it was painful and distressing at the time, the hospital was something of a respite. It certainly made my escape possible."

Edward and his mother quietly smiled at each other in complete understanding.

"Your father was diagnosed with vascular dementia some time ago. I reacted rather badly by overcompensating. I became so exhausted and depressed."

"Well, after my escape from hospital, and waking up back in my own room at home, I realised what was in-store for your father and me. I did not like it at all. I did not want to spend the rest of our days together just surviving and waiting, waiting for what? I knew there could still be more time for us to enjoy together. So I dropped my old ideas, safe clothes and values, pulled out your grandmother's old trunk, tried on her beautiful clothes and changed."

"The effect was incredible. I felt a completely different person, strong and courageous. All in a day I moved to collect your father from the nursing home, organised money from the bank, phoned everyone who needed to know and left. We had always wanted to live in France, so it seemed obvious that we should go to St Pancras station, catch a train to Paris before going down to the south."

"We met Hellen on St Pancras station, immediately becoming friends and ending up travelling with her to Paris.

We gladly accepted her invitation to join her at her aunt's house, and here we are."

Ivy looked jubilant, so alive. Edward was amazed; he had definitely underestimated his mother. They kissed before going to their separate rooms to rest. All this emotion was exhausting, and they had to consider the options open to them.

Later that evening, over an extended delicious meal the like of which Edward had seldom tasted, and of course much delicious wine, he began to unwind. Changing out of his city suit helped. Conversation flowed as sweetly as the wine. Hellen looked at him with new eyes. He was not particularly handsome, yet he had a good face which opened up when he smiled. She could hardly see his eyes hidden behind those pretty severe glasses, but he was tall, slim and moved well. In casual clothes he looked quite different, rather nice actually.

As they all enjoyed the meal and each other, she realised he was intelligent, rather funny and he obviously loved his mother. Edward was a great hit with Sophie, he had spent some time in Paris, spoke French rather well and greatly enjoyed teasing this delightful elderly lady. She was also delighted to see her favourite niece so completely relaxed in his company. Ivy and Arthur were just happy to be there together with their son. Scruffy sat under the table ever hopeful.

The next day, a not to be forgotten day, the household came to life rather late. Ivy awoke, having slept long and deeply. She could hear the excited barking of Scruffy below her window and Arthur's shrieks of pleasure. She could smell coffee, wonderful coffee and slipping into her Mother's silk dressing gown, she went down to the kitchen. She found hot croissants and coffee waiting on the stove. Edward and Hellen were happily washing up together from the previous night.

She could see Sophie relaxing in the garden. Taking her croissant and coffee outside, she joined her.

"So good to be here, such a wonderful place," she murmured.

"So good to have you here, and what a delightful son you have."

"Yes, he is good. It's great to have his support. But now sadly we must continue our journey to the South. Of course it will be much easier with Edward to help, but I shall miss you."

"I shall miss you too, I have so enjoyed having you here," Sophie said with feeling.

"When we have found ourselves in the South, I will phone and you can join us there. It should not be too long." And the ladies knew that it would not be too long.

The washing-up completed Edward and Hellen joined them in the garden. It was another blissful morning, the sunlight filtering through the leaves of the apple tree and the garden seats waiting to be filled. With nothing amiss, they all sank peacefully into this little Eden thinking their own thoughts.

Edward broke the silence, "We must leave now. It's really been wonderful to meet you Sophie. Your incredible generosity and kindness to my parents I shall never forget. Thank you for everything." Everyone was quiet as they absorbed what Edward was saying. It was time that they left, but no one wanted it. An hour later a taxi arrived at the garden gate.

Was it really less than 24 hours since Edward arrived at that same gate? So much had passed between them. But, Arthur was missing. They looked everywhere for him, he was not to be found – not in the house, not at the end of the garden, all his favourite places were empty. Where could he be? They became really concerned. Scruffy gave them away in the end. They were hiding behind Sophie's old car at the back of her garage.

Arthur wanted to stay; he was distraught at having to part with Scruffy. He found so many excuses not to go, but it was no good, their journey had to continue. Hellen's promises to bring Scruffy down very soon helped to calm the situation. Arthur did love that scruffy dog. Why had he become so attached to this dog? Ivy knew. She decided to put it to the back of her mind.

The journey down to the south in a magnificent train was quite an experience. It had such comfortable seats and wide windows. Ivy could see mile after mile of open countryside.

This country was so big! Sporadic villages appeared at intervals, with a church spire always dominating. Small farms with an odd cow and a single horse grazed in the distance. There were few people to be seen. Where were they? They were certainly going into the unknown.

Chapter 8
Moving On

Sophie had packed a large picnic basket and as they investigated the contents their solemn mood evaporated. Arthur and Edward fell on a ripe Brie while Ivy delighted in a delicious piece of smoked eel. There were hams, chicken, homemade tarts, and so much fruit. Large shiny blue/ black grapes, small yellow pears and fleshy purple figs were all there to be found. Wonderful! All this was washed down with Sophie's favourite wine. What a picnic!

They were soon joined by a boisterous family, a mother, father, two teenage children with Grandma and a baby. The journey continued with them all sharing their picnics and joining in endless English/French speak all accompanied by much laughter and singing.

Ivy marvelled at the warm acceptance everyone had for one another. The family with the very old, the young, mother and father with the baby passed around like a parcel to be kissed and caressed by everyone. The baby landed on Ivy's lap. It was a happy baby, smiling and gurgling. Ivy liked having a baby on her lap after so many years, even if it smelt a bit. The noise! So much noise from the chattering and laughter. Everyone was having a great time and of course Arthur loved it. The helpful train assistants were charming and polite. In fact, it seemed to Ivy that most French people were charming and polite.

Eventually the three tired travellers arrived in Aix en Provence. The station was just as busy as Ivy's memories of St Pancreas Station. Was it less than a week ago? This French station looked and smelt very different.

Ivy was left standing alone while Edward and Arthur sorted out a hire car and hotel. She watched people meeting people, such joy and arm waving. She watched people leaving with much hugging, kissing and tears. And there were people just standing, waiting like herself, but not like herself. They were more colourful, less restrained. Ivy liked what she saw.

It was not long before Edward returned with Arthur in a small hire car. They had maps in hand and were ready for the road. It was evening, the late sun was going down, yet it was still warm. Soon they were organised into a very pleasant hotel devouring much needed steak and 'frites'. Then, thankfully it was off to bed. Arthur opted to sleep with Edward in one room leaving Ivy in another. Ivy felt alone. Why did Arthur her loving husband want to sleep with Edward? She felt somewhat jealous, abandoned, but this feeling soon passed as she remembered the problems with dementia. She was just being silly! She also realised that she was missing Sophie. She fell asleep smiling.

The next day was different. Instead of Sophie's big warm kitchen the three sat down to breakfast in a dining room, with help yourself arrangements. Not very inviting, but the croissants were good, also the coffee. Arthur quickly left their table, he wanted to join the other tables being completely unaware that few of the other guests understood a word of his English. In fact, his very presence seemed to make everyone happy.

"We have to find somewhere to rent soon," advised Edward,

"And it has to be in the country with lovely views," added Ivy.

On the long road east from Aix travelling to an unknown destination, excitement touched our three travellers. There were few cars on the road, only a few dilapidated trucks driven very slowly by even older small men. An occasional village could be seen in the distance and derelict farms. There were also fields upon fields of flowers. Ivy did not know their names, but she did know 'sunflowers' when she saw them. Ivy breathed in the warm air overwhelmed by the sweet smells surrounding her and being with the very people she so loved.

They started singing, all the old-fashioned songs of her youth. "Daisy, Daisy, give me your answer do," and, "You are my sunshine."

"Just like the adventures we used to have when you were boys," she said.

"But no Cornish pasties," added Edward.

Slowly the terrain changed, and they began to climb up into the hills where a few isolated sheep munched on the grass. Down a road full of potholes and wild flowers, they saw an empty cafe selling coffee and ice creams. They stopped outside, soon drinking coffee sitting in the sun. Arthur ran off to explore. In France they did not worry about his unusual behaviour. In England he had been something of a problem.

Ivy and Edward sat at peace looking at the empty road before them.

In time Arthur returned to show off a beautiful green frog he had found. It was beautiful, but they needed to continue their journey so they said another 'adieu'. As they continued upwards, the terrain became more rugged and the roads became narrower. Large boulders had to be circumvented and precipices avoided. Ivy could not look. She did not come to France to die.

A small village appeared not far above them suffused in sunlight.

"Stop, please stop, Edward. I must look around," called Ivy. They were overwhelmed by the huge vistas laid out before them. They saw hills terraced with vines, gnarled olive trees, mountains, valleys, streams and rivers. They could see for mile after mile. All they could hear were birds, the buzzing of insects and 'baaing' of sheep in the distance. They noticed that the air, still warm had become fresher. And they looked up at the blue, blue sky, with not a single cloud in sight. This was heaven on earth.

They entered the village over narrow cobbled streets, the stone houses stood close together, their doors open wide. Old women in black were seated in doorways, others were sitting together cheerfully chatting in the square, unconcerned by children running about their feet. Dogs, assorted dogs of unknown origin, were lying under bushes and cats slunk about.

"I really like this village. It's bigger than we thought. It has a lovely church with a spire going up to heaven," remarked Ivy.

"It also has a few shops, a charcuterie and a boulangerie," noted Edward.

They bought some baguettes, fruit and mouth-watering cheese. They planned a picnic on the grassy slope where they had stopped on the way up. They had to see that amazing sight again. They found the perfect place, sat down to their feast before falling asleep.

In time Edward awoke leaving his sleeping parents to make his way back to the village to investigate further. Quite quickly he came across the town hall which was open for business. Its main function being to sell property, for there were a great many houses for sale in that village. Edward left, having made great friends with the Mayor, with sheets of paper and a map covered in crosses. He felt really excited, rushing back to Ivy and Arthur to share his dream with his parents.

"Come on, come on and wake up. I've got a surprise. We are going house-hunting!"

Chapter 9
Decisions Decisions

Back in the village they arranged to stay at the only inn surrounded by flowers. They were welcomed with such warmth, and the smells emanating from the kitchen were mouth-watering.

"It's small but it will do very well while we look around, but we must get back in time for dinner," said Edward, sniffing the air.

"Now we go exploring," said Arthur.

Walking through the village, they saw several empty houses, mostly boarded up and for sale and they wondered why? "We have to go higher if we want views," insisted Ivy.

So they trudged on up a narrow winding track that seemed to lead nowhere.

Then they saw it. A large yellow stone farmhouse standing alone. It was very old with lots of outbuildings, some crumbling, some not, but in a perfect place overlooking the village and valleys beyond. Ivy knew instantly that this wonderful place was to be her home.

She stood there quietly absorbing the incredible views, mile upon mile of uninterrupted terrain, rugged hillsides and valleys were spread out before her. Would this really be her home? Edward and Arthur could not wait to investigate. The farmhouse had perfect proportions, yet it was near derelict, had broken windows and doors, uneven stone floors and a badly leaking roof. It was obvious that no one had lived there for years. The surrounding gardens where completely overgrown, but someone had loved them once. On clambering over an old stone wall, they were met by row upon row of high terraces. This had been a vineyard; the old vines overgrown but still making their presence felt. Arthur and Edward were overjoyed.

"This is it, Mum! This is heaven."

"But seriously could we live here? And could we cope with restoring such a wreck however beautiful it may be?" he continued.

Ivy had never seen her son look happier and she was not to be deterred.

"Of course we can, first we deal with the barn in the best condition and live there while the house is sorted out. Already there is a huge functioning kitchen. The kitchen is in really good order, it could be lived in right now, and the rest will follow." Ivy did not hesitate.

"What a job! What a wonderful job," gasped Edward.

Returning to the town hall they found it still open. The Mayor, short, bespectacled and past his sell-by-date was barely able to see above the papers on his desk, yet he was very much aware of his importance in the village. As he surveyed these crazy English people, he was scarcely able to believe his luck. He pointed out that nobody wanted the farmhouse anymore so if they really wanted to buy it, there would be no problems. He thought it best to pull it down. They could of course take possession immediately. There was just a question of money.

It did not take long to agree. The Mayor was delighted. He also knew that his wife would be even more delighted.

Ivy and Edward felt somewhat stunned – they had just agreed to buy a dream.

Edward had known for a long time that he was disenchanted with city life. Were all the stresses and strains worth it? At first, he had been appalled by his redundancy. He had felt such a failure, then his wife had left him for his best friend. At the time he had no idea what to do, now he did. He had received a good compensation package and could pay for the farm outright. He should have left the city years ago but had too much invested in it, and not enough courage! Now in this perfect place he could breathe, yet he did realise the huge step he was taking. He was still reasonably young and active. He fully understood that true happiness comes from doing something you really care about and not least the joy of caring for ones you love. He realised how Ivy was really precious to him and he loved her deeply.

When they returned to the *auberge* for a meal, they were surprised to see that it was full of people, all chattering and laughing. Children were running around the tables being chased by a small boy on an even smaller tricycle. Apparently it was his birthday. There was no menu; course after course just kept arriving in front of them. They had little idea of what they were eating, but as it was washed down with quantities of the local wine, it soon began to taste marvellous. A few people spoke broken English. Yet with Edward's fairly fluent French and with Arthur and Ivy's school French, they had a hilarious evening, going to bed very happy, and very late. While the daylight held, the locals began a game of boules outside but our English family were far too tired to be kept awake by the sounds of metal on metal.

The following day a family council meeting was necessary. Edward was concerned that he might have rushed his parents into something they might regret. So, after breakfast, sitting outside on the terrace shaded by fronds of yellow flowers, he began seriously.

"How are you feeling folks?"

"Marvellous," replied his mother casually.

"I like it here," replied his father.

"Do you think I am quite mad buying a dilapidated wreck of a farm?" Edward queried.

"Of course not, it's wonderful, we love it and never want to leave." replied Ivy.

"Well, we don't have to, but someone has to go back to England to sort out our affairs," said a very serious sensible Edward.

"Oh, Edward! Will you? Your father and I just can't imagine going back to our old life, anyway we can't face the journey," she added with a twinkle in her eye.

Edward agreed to return to England for a few days. He would see his brother, put his flat on the market, and go down to Exeter to collect some of his mother's most treasured possessions. She did not want much, only the photograph albums she had kept for years, and a few of his father's drawings.

"I think you should put our house on the market for us. I never wish to go back there again, too many painful memories," continued Ivy.

Arthur agreed, he never wanted to leave this haven in the hills. So Edward left his elderly parents in a strange place, in a strange land, which was now their land, promising to return in a week. They were content.

Chapter 10
Edward Returns

The journey back to London was good. The speeding TGV was amazing. It was so very quiet certainly giving Edward time for reflection. He had been made redundant, given quite a sum to compensate, so the purchase of the farm was not outrageous. There would be enough to renovate it and live for a couple of years. What then? He would leave that to fate, thinking on another day. Anyway, he would put his flat on the market, give half the proceeds to Valerie, his distant disenchanted wife, and be free. He really relished the idea of being free, after so many years of being bowed down by the responsibilities of a difficult controlling wife and two children. The two boys were independent now, living their own lives. He seldom saw them, they certainly would not mind him moving to France. They loved France, and it was an easy journey now. He might actually see more of them.

Coming out of the station into central London the overcast weather seemed to permeate his very soul, and the noise, so much traffic so many people! He rang his brother, they arranged to meet at 6p.m. for an early drink. He had over an hour to spare so wandered around the places he knew so well, walking down past the British Museum, across Trafalgar Square, then down Piccadilly to his club. London was certainly overcast and grey, but the buildings were always impressive. Would he miss them?

At his club he picked up The Times, settled into a comfortable chair and waited for his brother.

He liked his brother, they had much in common – sport, children, work, but what else? Edward pondered, 'When did he last go to a museum or a concert?' London had so much to offer, he seldom went to anything, and perhaps he would do more from the south of France.

His thoughts were interrupted by a stylish man in a smart grey suit with briefcase coming towards him. It was Tony, his brother.

"Edward how good to see you. Have you got them and how are they?"

Edward smiled and took a few deep breaths before answering.

"No, Tony, I have not got them, I have left them in Provence where they are happily ensconced in a charming little *auberge*. And I have bought a derelict farmhouse there. It's wonderful." He looked so happy. Tony had to pause while taking it in.

"Edward, it all sounds incredible, but how are you going to manage financially? And do you realise what you are doing, saddling yourself with two old people, one of whom has Alzheimer's?"

"Yes, I do, Tone. Mum is amazing, she's suddenly got strong, and you would scarcely recognise her. She and I simply love it down there, together I think we can cope with Dad. They have a wonderful relationship as you know, it just shines through. I really admire her. By the way, they have sorted out her hip, she's no longer limping or in pain."

"Anyway, I plan to sell the flat, give half to Valerie, use my bit to do up the farmhouse and survive for a couple more years. I have no idea what I shall do but it all will be an adventure, something will happen. I do know one thing Tony, I never want to go back to the city, and I never want to wear a pin-stripe suit ever again"

Tony paused to take this all in. He was glad he was not wearing his pin-striped suit.

Edward walked back to his flat through the streets that held so many memories. He had been in love once, it seemed a very long time ago. Where had it all gone? The years, the children had certainly left their mark, Valerie leaving was a shock, he would never have left her, he was in it for the long haul. He thought the long haul had obviously been too much for her. Edward walked up the steps to his flat rather dreading the emptiness he would find there. He turned the key, walked through the door and was met by the sound of music and laughter coming from his kitchen. Incensed, he walked towards the sound throwing open the door. He saw his wife joyously embracing his best friend. He went no further. Returning to the sitting room, he sat down in his favourite armchair to recover and waited. Valerie walked out of the kitchen first, with his old friend at her heels. "What are you doing here Edward? I thought you had gone to France to pick up your mum." She was strident, controlled and exquisitely casual.

"Well, I'm not in France, and am not, as you say picking up my mum. I went over there imagining that she needed my help but she didn't. She is living with my father in Provence. They are both extremely happy. I shall be joining them just as soon as I have sold this flat."

Valerie was horrified, raising her voice.

"But you can't. I like this flat, I like it here. Anyway, I have secured a new highly paid job and it's terribly convenient."

"So what do you propose?" said Edward thoughtfully.

"Well, I'm going to stay here, so you have a problem. I'm not moving out, there is no way I could ever live with you again. Best friend likes it too, so I suggest you leave." Edward considered. He knew what he wanted, he had had a long train journey to decide. He felt strong, standing up, he looked his wife straight in the eye.

"Number one, I will sign over the flat to you my dear, if you make no further demands on me. You can keep the contents."

"Number two, you better know that I will no longer be working in the city, so no maintenance."

"Number three, I intend to move to the south of France and live on my capital for a bit."

"Number four, I give you until tomorrow morning to consider this very generous offer. I shall be staying with my brother until 10 o'clock tomorrow morning."

"I shall then take the train down to Exeter to sort out our parents' affairs."

With that he walked across the room, bade them both goodbye, leaving his wife and best friend stunned. This was not the placid Edward of yesteryear.

Of course, his brother and his wife welcomed him as he landed on their doorstep, they also welcomed the news that Valerie, erstwhile wife, would like to take over his flat. They were sure that she would, it was a very generous offer and her new job came with a considerable salary. Edward felt relieved. They all had an extremely convivial evening talking about the state of the economy, and things. Valerie had not been very popular with Edward's relations so no more was mentioned of her.

Sharp at 8 o'clock the next day, the phone rang. It was Valerie, she had accepted his terms.

Chapter 11
Scenes of Destruction

At 1 o'clock, Edward arrived at Exeter station. He made his way to the Cathedral, found his favourite restaurant nearby overlooking the Green and settled down with a coffee to relax. He had always loved this old part of Exeter, he particularly enjoyed looking over at the Cathedral. He delayed going to his parent's house; too many memories. Somehow he made his way into the Cathedral, he had not been there for many years. The magnificence of this ancient building seeped into him. Few people were there. The organ was playing in the background. He wandered around alone. He tried to pray, but it had been a long time since he had prayed. He just sat there at peace. It was utterly beautiful, having a permanence that his life had not. He was glad to be rid of his past life, yet he did not look forward to dismantling his parent's house, their lives and his childhood.

He pensively walked down the familiar road, past the village shop towards his old home. So many past events from his childhood crowded into his mind, making it difficult to concentrate on the task in hand.

He knew something was wrong before he got to the gate. There were bollards and police notices everywhere forbidding access. People were crowding around. He climbed over the cordons, nobody stopped him, quietly walking to number 34, his house, his parent's house. A scene of destruction met his eyes. A number 173 bus had swerved to avoid a dog, mounted the pavement, crashed through the garden fence, stopping only when confronted by his parents' marble fireplace having gone through their bay window. The police would not allow him to pass. It was not safe. He could see that the front lintel was hanging crazily, also smoke was rising from somewhere or other. Frightened and injured passengers were struggling to get out of the rear door of the bus, all shocked and fearful. Police were shouting, ambulance sirens were shrieking and a fire engine had just arrived. Edward's home as he knew it was no more. If he had been just a little earlier he would have been inside this scene of destruction. Instead, he had been sitting quietly in Exeter Cathedral. At that moment he really thanked God for his very life. He also became aware that Ivy and Arthur would have been in there if Ivy had not had the courage to leave taking that leap into the dark. He shook his head and walked away having given the police all his particulars.

Returning to London he let himself into his brother's flat, poured himself a very large whiskey, collapsed into a familiar armchair and fell asleep.

He awoke when his brother came crashing through the door.

"You're back early old thing. You must have put a spurt on. Did it all go well?"

"What a day, Tony! I am completely thrashed. I did not put a spurt on, too much chaos. The old home is a wreck. I'll explain later," answered Edward.

He accepted another whiskey from his thoughtful brother, beginning to unwind in the telling of the day's events. Tony's wife was out doing something or other so the brothers decided to go out for a meal at their favourite Italian restaurant. They had much to discuss, the insurance, the sealing up of the house, the repairs, finding builders and eventually estate agents. They realised that it was quite a project. It was decided that Edward would return to the south of France to sort out their parents. Tony would sort everything else out in England. These brothers really understood each other, easily organising what each one would do. They had shared a childhood and felt the organic tug of family. They stood up, bade each other goodbye, shook hands and went their separate ways.

Travelling down to the south of France was uneventful, giving Edward time to consider his options. He was surprised to find that despite all the problems that surrounded him he felt happy, really happy. The next part of his life was going to be an adventure, he loved adventures.

When he arrived back at the *auberge* in his tiny hire car he felt that he had come home. He could see his parents sitting in the shade in deep conversation with a man in black. Edward chortled, his rather subdued parents in England were certainly blossoming in their new environment. The sun shone down as they laughed and chattered to a stranger like old friends. Edward joined them. Ivy was so pleased to see her son again.

"Edward, you're back! We didn't expect you for a couple more days. This is Father Dominique, he looks after the church here, has spent some time in Rome and England and he speaks really good English. He is going to teach us to speak French. In fact, we have picked up some words already."

Ivy's enthusiasm was infectious and the priest was happy to join them in a bottle of Beaujolais. He told them that he said Mass most days at 10 o'clock, and they were very welcome. On Sundays it was 11 o'clock. He was a Catholic priest, but Ivy did not hold this against him. It did not bother her what religion anyone practised, or indeed if they practiced none at all.

"Yes, yes of course we will come, but you must know that we are C. of E. and haven't been to church in years," she said.

The priest just smiled.

"You will like my church, most of the locals come, and it's a good way of meeting them. Of course it will improve your French," he said with cheerful irony.

The priest knew everyone. Edward encouraged him to talk about his life. Father Dominique really enjoyed speaking expansively of his memories of England and abroad. Hours passed. When the priest left, Edward knew where to find the most reliable garage, he also knew of the best builders, gardeners and stonemasons. Ivy knew where to find the market, a hairdresser's and a shoe shop. Ivy could meet all the other ladies in the church on Sunday. Someone would help her in the house.

On reflection, Ivy felt at a loss, her French was really not up to holding any sort of conversation with her neighbours or indeed buying anything from the local shops. What could she do?

Chapter 12
A Sensible Car

Edward left early the following morning with plans to buy a good sensible car. The hire car was too expensive to keep for any length of time and far too small.

The sun was shining, the birds were singing, and all was well in the world. A gentle warmth embraced him as he smiled at the villagers who smiled back. All felt idyllic as he drove slowly through the village looking for the recommended garage on the far side.

The garage looked pretty rough, with rusty tin roof, this dilapidated building had carcasses of ancient cars lying in heaps all around the place. Open doors hanging from rusty hinges and enormous tires lay haphazardly on the ground. Edward hesitated, he began to doubt the priest's recommendation. He walked tentatively towards the buildings. A thin wild looking dog on a long chain barked at him menacingly. He did not like the place or the dog, and where was everyone? It was all very quiet, except for the dog's persistent barking.

"What sort of place is this? Where is everyone?" shouted Edward.

"Hello, hello," he shouted again and again. No response.

He made his way through the old building avoiding the bits of engines and exhaust pipes strewn across the way. All the windows were broken and huge cobwebs hung from the roof. The pungent smell of oil permeated the whole building.

At last Edward spied a very old man lying under a sort of truck completely involved in its repair.

"Hello, hello," he called out again.

The old man, thin, brown and wrinkled responded with a faint toothless grin. Nothing else.

His face was black with oil and soot, his large brown ears acted as barricades to prevent the thin strands of oily hair from falling into his small dark eyes. He was skinny, definitely skinny, looking quite extraordinary in a filthy dark blue boiler suit that had once fitted a much larger man.

"Bonjour, monsieur. Comment ça va?" ventured Edward. So this is the best garage around, thought Edward.

"I need to buy a new car, the priest sent me," he said.

"Parfait, Celui-ci c'est parfait pour vous," was the old man's reply, pointing to the truck.

"No. No, said Edward, somewhat horrified,

"I want a really good car."

"Mais je vous assure, elle best parfaite. It is very good for you and the priest recommended it," replied the small man in the large hanging boiler suit.

There was no disputing this, nor the old man's determination to sell him that dreadful old machine up on the ramp. He would deliver it the following day.

Edward accepted that this was all there was on offer driving slowly back to the village, rather unsure about his first purchase in his new life. But what could he do? The priest had recommended it. The following day Edward was rather relieved when the new vehicle did not arrive.

Ivy had organised a picnic so they set off to further investigate the farm, their future home. It was as they remembered, so beautiful that it almost took their breath away. The silence was awesome, broken only by the song of a skylark overhead and the hum of bees. They wandered around breathing in the atmosphere and thinking their own thoughts. Arthur was the first to break the spell jumping up shouting to the world.

"I love it, I love it here!" while scrambling up a hill nearby, his laughter echoing behind him.

Ivy and Edward did not want to move or indeed speak as they sat in the sun listening to the murmuring of spring and inhaling the scent of wildflowers.

In time, Arthur returned staggering with armfuls of wild flowers. Coming straight towards Ivy he threw them down at her feet.

"For you," he said, an enormous smile spreading across his face, then he ran away.

Ivy with great care, picked them up her heart bounding with love for this man who had always been by her side.

The old farmhouse was really neglected and would surely have fallen apart had they not bought it. There were many tiles missing from the roof, a tree was actually growing through the floor of the main living room, its branches breaking through one of the windows. Dark green damp patches covered the walls and the only bathroom had completely fallen off the side of the house.

Were they mad to take this on? The only room that was habitable was the enormous kitchen with a nasty old black range along one side. Ivy was enchanted.

"Wonderful, wonderful my grandmother had a cooker just like this! She cooked amazing meals for her entire family on it. All we need are pots and pans and a large table of course. That is all we need."

She ran up to it and touched it reverently. Edward doubted his mother's enthusiasm.

"You really mean to cook on that thing?" he said.

"Yes," she replied adamantly staring into his eyes.

"All it needs is a good clean and blacking. Its market day in the village tomorrow so we must do some shopping."

That said, it was all arranged.

On further inspection, they found that one of the old barns was in surprisingly good shape. It even contained a few rusty old beds. The roof didn't leak and there were no damp walls here. Yet no bathroom.

'How odd! Someone has lived here quite recently, yet how could anyone live without a bathroom?' reflected Ivy.

She found some sort of loo in a small shed some distance away while Edward found a water tap attached to a tree. He was delighted when dirty brown water spilled out, obviously used for washing hands and animals.

"This is good enough really," he said.

"But we need clean water and a proper bathroom," added Ivy firmly.

"I will soon get you a bathroom, Mother," Ivy thought he was being rather hopeful.

Walking around the outhouses they could see that there had been chickens in one of the barns with nesting boxes. There was a shed that had been used for goats, their names scrawled above the doors. They did not really want goats, at least not yet. Then there were pigsties. They really did not want pigs either. They went on to an out-house near the main house which had a built-in copper and a mangle. Another delight for Ivy, as she remembered helping her mother on a Monday morning with the washing. She had loved turning the handle of the mangle as a child, but on inspection this mangle had had it. The rubber had completely deteriorated.

"We will just have to put up a washing line and buy pegs," she said.

"We can make a prop, there is enough wood lying around here to build another house!" enthused Edward. Overwhelmed by the excitement their project offered, they collapsed onto the grassy bank again for another picnic.

"I don't miss tea at all, I used to love tea at 4 o'clock drinking from my grandmother's china tea cups," mentioned Ivy. On reflection she did feel a little sad at the loss of her grandmother's porcelain teacups.

Later, much later they returned to the auberge where monsieur and madam were waiting outside to welcome them. "It is good that you buy the big farmhouse, it is a good place. Bravo!"

They hugged Edward and Arthur at length, and kissed Ivy profusely on both cheeks, then again and again, their enthusiasm was boundless.

"Bravo, bravo we need a celebration!"

The entire village seemed to be squeezed into the Auberge that evening. They were in the hall, in the dining room, the salon, all spilling out onto the terrace and beyond. Ivy knew that she had never been kissed so much in her entire life. Sadly, she did not understand a word of all the greetings. She did however understand the real warmth which surrounded her, all ages, men women and children including the tricyclist still in evidence going in and out of the tables and people's legs. All was so joyful.

Chapter 13
The Street Market

Arthur particularly liked the Auberge and he really liked helping out in the kitchen, feeding the rabbits, collecting eggs from the chickens, and he also liked madame.

The tiny hire-car was too small for the intended shopping expedition so it was decided that he would stay at the auberge.

Monsieur was driving into town that day in his spacious Mion truck, of which he was very proud, so Ivy and Edward went with him. Down the winding mountain track they drove, with this wild Frenchman at the wheel. He drove so fast with sheer drops either side. Ivy sank further and further into her seat, shut her eyes, prayed and hoped. Edward sat up stoically hanging on to a sidebar. He was hoping, too.

They arrived in town by 10 a.m., going straight to a café where the *aubergist* greeted all his friends enthusiastically joining them in tossing back brandy after brandy. Ivy and Edward left them to it, there was no way they could toss back brandy at 10 o'clock in the morning.

When they entered the main square, they were met by so many people all talking at the top of their voices, so much noise and so much colour!

They were thrilled by everything they saw. They bought cleaning materials, rope, pegs, a hammer, nails and a hose pipe. To Ivy's surprise, Edward also bought a large tin bath, several rolls of plastic sheeting and a staple gun. Moving on through the market they found boxes of assorted china, and lots of mixed cutlery, saucepans, frying pans and casserole dishes. Next it was tablecloths and rolls of dark blue check material.

The food market was next, Ivy was intoxicated by the sight of so many different things. There were live rabbits in cages, tiny song birds in even smaller cages and a rather poor looking puppy. Ivy wanted to save them all. She knew their ultimate destinations.

There were so many different types of olives, big and fat, small and black, and so many different mushrooms! Ivy was not at all sure that she wanted to buy these decidedly foreign species! There were quantities of exotic fruit. Wonderful vegetables piled high on tressel tables had come in from the country that day. The ancient-looking farmer with back half bent, a starved-look on his deeply etched brown face, somehow smiled at her. Ivy smiled in return. She instinctively knew this half-starved look, feeling real compassion for him. Huge heaps of melons lay around on the bare earth. A boy with a bicycle, too old to be ridden, staggered past with hundreds of plaited onions hanging from the handlebars. There were more on a central bar to the back and more stacked into the huge box at the rear.

'How could he ever manage to push this bike?' Ivy wondered.

Ivy felt battered by so many conflicting interests and so much emotion.

After everything was packed onto the truck they had to wait for a surprise that Edward had found.

"What is it?" Ivy asked.

Edward would not say. He just smiled.

Ivy did not have long to wait as coming towards them were four men carrying the heaviest, surely the biggest ancient oak table Ivy had ever seen, a perfect table for her new kitchen. She sighed with pleasure.

"Oh, Edward, what can I say? I love it, absolutely love it and I love you. Thank you, thank you so much. It's perfect."

She could not stop touching it quietly repeating, "It's perfect, Edward, it's perfect." Somehow, they managed to fit this very heavy piece of furniture into the back of the camion truck helped by many friends and much gesticulation retreating to their favourite cafe nearby. It was rather sparse with long tables covered in plastic cloths with old posters stuck on walls. Jugs of wine placed down the centre of the tables were just waiting for thirsty customers. They sat down to recover enjoying much wine and a hot sustaining meal. It was all very cheerful, very raucous with everyone talking at once. Ivy sat bemused, grateful to leave the talking to Edward.

The journey back to the *auberge* was certainly not as fast as the journey down. It was laden not just with Ivy's purchases but also with the enormous, extremely heavy table.

The truck was very unstable rocking about alarmingly. Monsieur was laughing and shouting volubly as he made it around the treacherous bends. It was fun, great fun, he had done this many times before.

At the *auberge*, Ivy staggered up to her bed. It had been quite an eventful morning. She slept soundly for several hours.

When she awoke, eager and refreshed, she went downstairs. There was no one there, no Arthur, no Edward, no monsieur, no madame, and no camion truck. She decided not to worry, sitting down outside on a large wicker armchair to rest some more, admiring her new world. Her only company was the cat of the house, who decided to jump onto her lap, talking to her in exquisite catty language.

It was getting late when Edward, Arthur and Monsieur reappeared, looking happy, relaxed, pretty dirty and very tired. They had delivered everything up to the farm with the help of a considerable number of ancient villagers, all soon reviving with liberal amounts of wine. Ivy considered that they had so many new friends now. She could hardly believe it, she had felt so lonely in England. Arthur was in his element, passing around drinks and chatting to the locals in his vastly improving schoolboy French. He seemed to be picking it up rather quicker than she was. Ivy decided to do something about it, she made a plan to see the Priest the following day.

Chapter 14
The Priest's House

The following day, Edward and Arthur decided to visit the garage again. "*C'est bien ca,*" Edward called out.

"*Demain, il faut que bien faire. Ca fait bien,*" was the reply. Edward felt helpless. This ancient village mechanic was adamant that he was selling Edward a really good vehicle. Edward was not so sure. He wondered if it would be with him the next day, or even the day after that, yet he left in good spirits. He rather liked this way of business, he actually liked the inefficiency. Father and son wandered back through the village, chatting aimlessly about nothing much, both happy to be in each other's company.

Ivy was missing when they returned. She had gone to see Father Dominique and would be back shortly.

Ivy arrived at the priest's rather large stone house next to the church. She noticed that it looked well cared for, the garden awash with flowers. Was it jasmine that she could smell from the gate? The entrance porch was covered in the tiny white flowers.

"Wonderful," she said aloud as she inhaled the heady scent.

Before she had a chance to knock on the door it was opened by Father Dominique himself, smiling as ever. "Welcome, welcome! How good to see you, come in, come in."

Ivy walked into a truly beautiful room with the stone floor polished like glass and a huge fireplace. And bookshelves overflowing with books everywhere!. There was a large oak desk at the far end of the room covered in papers with a seat nearby. A couple of comfortable armchairs on a worn Indian rug were placed by one of the windows. Ivy was bade to sit down.

"I will bring tea immediately," said the priest.

"Tea, tea in France, wonderful!" replied Ivy.

She looked at the big wooden cross hanging on the wall. A picture of the Virgin and Child hung above the desk. There were no other ornaments. She waited quietly in this cool peaceful room.

The priest returned bringing in tea on a large oval tray with delicate china cups and saucers. There were tiny rum doughnuts cooked by ladies of the village, and digestive biscuits. Ivy loved digestive biscuits. It was good to be here with this charming young man. He was probably about her sons' age, but she was no good at telling ages anymore. Whatever his age, he was rather handsome, with deep, enquiring eyes and wide smiling mouth. She wondered as to his past life. The tea was good, the conversation casual. Ivy was very happy to be there. At last she came to the purpose of her visit. "Father Dominique, I need your advice. This is the most wonderful place, I love it here but I am sad my French is so poor I can scarcely understand a word of these wonderful people who are our neighbours and friends."

Tears began to roll down her face as she hesitated, unable to say more, then she cried out:

"And Arthur, my darling husband Arthur, has Alzheimer's." There, she had said the dreaded word. The priest let her cry awhile, with pity in his heart for this brave little woman who had come to him for help.

"You have come to the right place. Dementia is a frequent visitor in old age, here we care for everyone affected. We allow them to get on with their lives as they understand it, and as a community we are there for them. You are not alone."

Ivy began to feel better, just having admitted her fear to another soul. She also realised that she missed Sophie. The priest quietly suggested that she might give English lessons at the school. He would provide cards with pictures in words in French and English. In that way she would get involved in the village, learning French by the way. Ivy was not at all sure about this but was willing to try. It was arranged that she would be introduced to the school mistress the next day. She walked back to the *auberge* with a lighter step, contemplating her new life and her new job. She would phone Sophie.

Sophie was delighted to hear from her. Ivy could not stop talking, she was so enthusiastic so much had happened to her. Would Sophie like to join them?

"Of course, my dear, I will arrive in about a week. In the meantime, I have to put my house to bed. I embrace you. The days will pass very quickly."

Chapter 15
The Heap Arrives

The new vehicle, a sort of truck, arrived at 8 a.m. It certainly looked ramshackle, with not much paint and a great deal of rust, Edward nevertheless was pleased to see it, no more a tiny hire-car that he had begun to dislike intensely. He felt that this new vehicle would probably be able to get up the mountainside even if it looked pretty ancient, coughing and spluttering rather a lot. This truck was the answer. Having thanked and paid for it, he listened to his new friend from the garage cordially singing the vehicle's praises before embracing him and wishing him and it well. Edward certainly hoped the truck would do well.

Arthur and Ivy packed themselves into the front of the heap, as Edward called it, at 8.30 a.m. They needed more essentials. Edward drove down to the village somewhat more tentatively than Monsieur. With Sophie arriving before long, they needed to sort out their living arrangements. They wanted to move away from the *auberge* into their own home, whatever state it was in. Beds and mattresses were necessary, pillows, duvets and towels, along with soaps, brooms, buckets and mops, disinfectants and weed-killers. What had they taken on! They also needed aprons, overalls, and strong working shoes. Ivy's mother's shoes looked rather worn now.

The market had not changed. It was still chaotic with even more people noisily hassling to buy the best food. These French ladies knew nothing about queuing or not touching the ripe fruit carefully set out before them. Eventually, they found themselves in the antique shop again where Edward had discovered Ivy's kitchen table. This time they bought an assortment of wooden chairs, an armoire, a couple of heavy oak dressers and a dressing-table perfect for Ivy's new bedroom. All these things would be delivered the following day. It was quite amazing; shopping was made so easy here. They stopped for lunch at the now familiar cafe with its trestle tables and carafes of wine waiting. They consumed another sustaining meal and drank another carafe of wine. All was well in the world. Ivy had never felt closer to her son than on that morning. She reflected that they were very alike, same humour, same courage, same compassion, but he did not look like her side of the family, more Arthur's, but that was O.K. She liked the look of her husband.

When they returned to the *auberge*, Ivy sank into the now familiar wicker chair dozing off under the olive tree. She awoke to find that all was quiet with only Cat for company. Ivy noted that the cat put in an appearance only when the men were out of sight. The cat jumped onto her lap snuggling up close to her. Ivy had never much liked cats but she liked this one. Was it because he liked her? Probably, she mused. At dusk, so many villagers in so many trucks disturbed her peace. They had all been working on the farm with Edward and Arthur.

So much had been achieved, it had all been such fun, with another party spilling out of the *auberge*. Ivy loved these people who included her in their world. The isolation she had felt in her past life was gone. Throwing her arms up into the air she called out to the mountains above

"I love it here. I do so love it here. Thank you, thank you God!"

It transpired that the roofer had fixed the roof, the stonemason had repaired the end of the farmhouse and was coming back tomorrow to sort out the windows of the kitchen. The walls, floor and larder had been scrubbed, all would be ready for painting the next day. Many huge tins of white paint had arrived from somewhere, also large brushes just waiting to transform her new home. All the workforce said it would be perfect in a month, certainly habitable in a week. Ivy hoped they were right. Sophie was coming in a week. She said nothing, secretly thinking it impossible, but she was ever hopeful.

The following morning, Edward, with his friendly builders, gathered outside to go up to the farm. Arthur had been waiting outside in the truck since dawn.

Edward looked for his mother who was still in bed. "Dearest Ma, leave us for a couple of days to get the heavy stuff out of the way, then come up to tell us what you would like," he spoke softly. Ivy was grateful.

"Of course, darling. I don't mind a bit. Anyway, I am going to the schoolmistress's house today. The priest says I should meet her."

The schoolmistress was a tall angular woman of uncertain age who lived in a sort of shoebox next to the school. Ivy noted that she had to bend almost double to get through the door. Although she looked like a stick, she was a cheerful stick, Ivy liked her immediately. She spoke reasonably good English and smiled a lot.

"I am thrilled that you wish to help me with my children," she said. Ivy was not quite so sure.

"I hardly speak French, I have never taught before," she offered.

"Zat is good, ve ve good, we vill 'av fun. Come, see my family."

Her family, her school children, were of mixed ages, from about five to 10 years old. There were about 20 of them, seated on long benches outside the school room. They all looked so good, waiting for instructions of the day. Ivy was introduced. Each one came forward formally to shake her hand and thank her for joining them.

"*Merci, madame, tres, tres gentil,*" they all said.

They were so polite, even the small boy on the trike who had terrorised the others at the *auberge*. He looked like a little angel. They were certainly not like the children she came across in England. But were they always so perfect? She was very pleased that the stick-lady was to be with her at the beginning.

Chapter 16
Ivy Waits

Three days passed before Ivy joined the men in one of the trucks going up the hill. She sat in the front of Edwards new heap squeezed between Edward and Arthur with Edward singing the praises of this new toy! He loved his truck! They proceeded in a sort of convoy, a very noisy convoy; there were several vehicles. Ivy could not look, as they drove on the very edge of the unmarked road round the horrifying bends. She supposed she would get used to it.

When they reached the farm Ivy was flabbergasted, so much had changed. The rubble was mostly gone, just an orderly pile left. All the doors had been fixed, no more hanging and banging in the wind. The holes in the roof had been repaired and immaculately re-tiled. The rotten windows were replaced and even the walls looked sort of straight. Someone was a really good stonemason.

Ivy could hardly speak.

"I can't believe it...you've done so much, and so quickly," she kept repeating.

"Just wait until you see inside the side barn," said Edward as he guided her towards the door.

All was white, white walls, white ceilings, even the stone floors, now scrubbed and polished looked white. Ivy walked through the hallway and up the stairs. She could see the morning sun streaming through open windows, everywhere was infused with golden light. The bedrooms, now white, had beds and mattresses in place. The far one at the end, the biggest with windows on two sides had a new huge window overlooking the wide sweep of hills beyond. A large, double bed was waiting for her.

"Wonderful, so wonderful," gasped Ivy.

Edward left her to assimilate it all. She had never imagined that anything so perfect could be hers!

Later when she came downstairs, she lingered looking around at so much beauty before her. Edward was waiting. "Come on, Ma, more to show you."

They walked together over the cobbled courtyard, towards the main house. Ivy had forgotten how big it was. It certainly looked imposing, somehow not the wreck of last week. Edward opened the back door, a heavy old oak door, with polished handles and hinges. What a door! Ivy walked through it into the most amazing kitchen, her kitchen. It was enormous. It had windows all along one side, and French doors onto a terrace at the far end. The table, her table was in the centre, with all the odd chairs arranged around it. Her stove, that big rusty stove that reminded her of her grandmother's house, was now standing resplendent, cleaned, blackened and alive with logs already burning inside. And the larder newly painted with slate shelves, was waiting for her to fill. Ivy sat down, she was speechless, unable to take it all in.

Arthur grabbed a yard-broom rushing out through the side-door to the dilapidated terrace. Ivy watched as he moved planks of wood, energetically sweeping around what was left of it. She saw he was making a proper terrace. He was so proud of himself pulling out an ancient grapevine. She watched as he swept away the rubble accumulated over the years, and she continued to watch as he covered himself in dirt and grime. He was so, so happy. She felt such pride as she looked at him.

A man needs something to do, even if his mind is slipping, she thought.

And as she watched, and as she thought, she realised how happy she felt, and how much she loved this man.

Chapter 17

A Problem

Water was a problem, all they had found was contaminated. They could manage the dark with candles, they could keep warm, at least in the kitchen by the range, but they needed water. Clean water to drink, to cook with, and to wash. They had found an old outside tap, which they had used for cleaning, but it gushed out rusty yellow water, and a water tap in the old laundry was just the same. It was not good enough. A water-diviner was needed.

The diviner arranged to come from a neighbouring village.

They could not move in without water. He arrived, a small bent man with deeply lined face. He was very thin and very brown. Ivy could see that everyone around her was pretty brown, even her son and husband were heading in that direction. She had not looked in a mirror for a week, she suspected that she was looking less white now too, even though she wore her newly acquired sun hat.

Edward and Ivy were acutely aware that if water could not be found then their dream would not materialise. Perhaps they should not have wanted the farm so much. It had all seemed so easy, everything falling into place as if pieces from a jigsaw, but the last piece was missing.

The water diviner was impressive. Without saying a word, he collected his sticks, his divining rods from the back of his old three-wheeler and walked purposefully to the slope behind the house. All work stopped, everyone gathered in awe to gaze at this extraordinary little man. He had the air of a witch doctor who held sway over the many tribes in Africa. This man, this agile monkey of a man, had power over a mountain, their mountain. They all watched respectfully waiting for a miracle to happen.

With arms stretched out before him this incredible man slowly covered the rocky ground behind the farm buildings. Would his rods find what they needed? Time passed. A long time passed. Everyone, including Ivy, watched and waited in silence.

"Will he really find water? What will we do if there is none?" Ivy whispered to Edward.

He put a comforting arm around his mother.

"Of course we will find water, he's the best there is. There used to be water here in the past. The diviner is looking for the water trapped under the rocks. It hails from a good source high up the mountain." Edward sounded knowledgeable.

Ivy waited and hoped. They all waited and hoped, standing in the sun for what seemed like hours.

And as time passed, they all began to feel despondent, yet the diviner was not to be disturbed. He was intent on his task.

"There has to be water here, there has always been water here, good drinking water," shouted a man from the crowd.

"I worked here all my life, and there was more than enough here then," added another.

"We had seven full-time workers, and many more at harvest time," others shouted.

The villagers all remembered, and their spirits raised. The diviner, unperturbed continued his slow concentrated task.

Dusk was beginning to set in. They all wanted to return to their homes, but the diviner would not be distracted. They continued to wait patiently, and in silence. Suddenly, a shout came out of the early evening gloom, like a bullet from a shotgun. Water was gurgling down the hillside towards them.

"He's really done it." whispered Ivy.

"*Ici!*" cried the diviner.

Men raced over the slope towards him, with pick-axes and shovels, immediately getting to work. They knew what to do. The water, so much water now, had to be controlled. Excitement filled the air.

"*Profondement!*" shouted the diviner.

The men dug deeper.

Suddenly it happened, great jets of water shot up into the air. There was cheering and hugging, everyone congratulating the diviner and of course, each other. The spring had been found and unblocked. They knew it would work. They all knew it would work. There was water again at Les Vergers.

Chapter 18
A Shower for Ivy

A week had passed. So much excitement and so much emotion had engulfed the ever-resilient Ivy.

She found herself lying in her soft enveloping bed at the *auberge* not wanting to get up or indeed leave it. She looked about her, the early morning sunshine filtered through the shutters of her room, her pretty white room with cosy floral eiderdown and simple country furniture. All was silent, all so peaceful. Ivy decided to stay in bed.

Several hours later, a tap on her door was followed by madame carrying a small tray of biscuits fruit juice and coffee. Madame was large in size and character, pleasantly round, in body and face, with a cheery expression and wide-open eyes. Ivy had never really looked at her before, with so much going on around her. Now she really looked at her hostess, really liking what she saw. This woman was lovely, not in a generally accepted way of beauty, but a natural beauty real contentment shining through. Ivy longed to speak to her as she bustled about opening up the shutters but could not find any words. Then this lovely lady pumped up the huge square pillows behind Ivy's head. "*Merci, madame. Beaucoup merci,*" was all Ivy could say. She felt impotent, more than ever determined to get a grip on the language.

Madame left, as quietly as she had entered.

Ivy had not had breakfast in bed since a child. She loved it. A note on her tray suggested she have a quiet day. Her son was considerate, he felt she really needed a quiet day. Up at the farm all was going to plan. The builders were continuing to build, excavating a well and fitting water-pipes down to the farm kitchen. The barns would have water the following day,

The men as always were creating great piles of rubble wherever they worked, nobody thought of clearing up, they were having far too much fun. Edward left them and their heaps of rubble. He would create a perfect place for Ivy to shower. He really wanted to move into the farm whatever the state of the buildings but knew that his mother would not be happy with no washing facilities. He decided to make a shower, putting it outside the newly restored barn. It would overlook the distant hills beyond. Edward really, really loved it here. He realised that he was moving more slowly now, and was becoming more tolerant. The Edward of old would not have put up with piles of rubble, now he did not mind, he rather liked the apparent chaos.

He began the task of creating some sort of shower, collecting planks of wood he found lying about outside. The struggle to put it all together was considerable, somehow he would manage to make it stay upright. First, he built a sort of wigwam, then he draped his roll of plastic sheet over it fixing it in place with his staples. All that was needed was time and patience, he thought. Perfection was not built in a day.

Making a door felt quite a complex thing to do so he left the front open. He knew that his mother would appreciate showering in the open air while overlooking such beauty. He lugged the old metal bath he had bought from the market into the enclosure. It did feel a bit exposed, so he went to the farmhouse kitchen found an old frying pan and a long metal spoon. He was going to make a gong. Delighted with his finds he took them back to his shower contraption hoisting the frying-pan up with rope onto the branch of an overhanging tree. Then he carefully placed the gong-spoon nearby. His mother could then bang on the frying pan with the spoon to let everyone know when she was in situ. She would like this very much.

This was a perfect shower, but as yet it had no water. He had seen an old watering can lying about in one of the garden sheds, so he cleaned it up, somehow fixing it high above the tin bath. He was very pleased with himself. The nozzle would form a perfect shower head. Unfortunately, Edward was not at all sure how to attach a water-pipe to the watering-can or indeed do the plumbing involved. He went off to find his friends the builders.

"*Facile, très facile,*" they all answered.

So a little procession of builders followed Edward to look at the problem.

"*Charmant, charmant,*" they said in unison.

"*Tres bien ca, maintenant tout bien fin de complete.*" They left, smiling, soon returning with an overflowing toolbox, a hosepipe and a good-looking tin water-tank which they had found lying about in the rubble. Edward was thrilled as he watched the men quickly sort out a water supply to his shower.

They said the water would heat with the rays of the sun.

Edward was completely happy.

Ivy quietly left the *auberge* to take a walk around the hillside. Wildflowers everywhere covered the land for miles. There were anemones, jonquils, hair-bells, wild roses, honeysuckle and many others she could not name, all wild, all beautiful, delicate and unbelievably fragrant. The air picked up the scent of not just the flowers but also herbs, so many herbs. Olives and figs grew along the overgrown track where she walked. She quietly made her way not wanting to disturb the perfect peace she found there. She saw a fallen log, sitting down she became completely aware of being part of all this. She walked on picking up the fallen figs on the way, eating them greedily, they were so delicious. She looked at the ancient olive trees, their extraordinary shapes fascinated her, she would plant some on the farm, but how long would they take to grow to any height? She did not know.

The track gradually became shaded by cypresses and it became cooler.

Suddenly the farmhouse appeared as if out of nowhere. It was much nearer the village than she had appreciated. She realised that she did not need transport to go down there anymore. She could walk, it felt good that she would be able to see the priest, the schoolmistress, and go to the *auberge* whenever she liked.

She made her way through the rubble towards her lovely kitchen, she just had to see it again. Someone was calling her. She looked around, Edward was waving enthusiastically.

"Here, Ma. Come over here. I've got something to show you."

"I've actually walked here, there's a track that comes up from the village, and it's full of ripe figs, olive trees, and wonderful flowers and things. I can't believe we are going to live here." Ivy could not stop talking.

"Ma, come and see; I've made something for you. I'm sure you will love it," said Edward.

Ivy followed her son to the back of the newly painted barn. A curious sort of arrangement covered in plastic, met her. "Isn't it wonderful! I've made you a beautiful new shower."

Edward was so excited by his endeavours that Ivy could only agree with him, but she did wonder if it would blow away in the wind, leaving her standing stark naked in an old tin bath.

"It's wonderful, Edward, I can't wait to try it out," said Ivy with some hesitation.

Chapter 19
So Many Chickens and a Black Cat

Now there was water at Les Vergers they decided it was possible to move in. Ivy's first priority was to buy some chickens, the rest would follow. They could buy essentials in the village but they needed fresh eggs. Madame at the *auberge* told them to go to see her cousin who would oblige. The next day Ivy, Edward and Arthur crammed into the front of the new truck. They drove up high into the mountains. They were getting used to the rough terrain, narrow roads which seemed to switch back every few yards, and the enormous rocks and potholes to navigate. Edward was driving faster now, as they all sang along happily. They had a few rough boxes in the back, twine and wire-netting, all the essentials they were told when buying chickens.

They could hear the farm before they got there.

"Chickens and ducks make a tremendous racket en mass," commented Edward.

Ahead was a large pond crammed with ducks, Aylesbury ducks, Call ducks, Indian runners, and mixtures, all quacking away like mad. Every type of chicken ran around, some big, some small, all shapes sizes and colours. And as they drove through this menagerie they saw goats, some tethered, some not. A couple of horses grazed in a field beyond with a contented black and white cow for company. Beyond flowers, fields and fields of blue, blue flowers.

"All so beautiful!" whispered Ivy.

Dogs came out of nowhere, racing towards them barking enthusiastically. What a welcome! Martha, the cousin, also came out to greet them, a baby in her arms, a small boy dangling behind her. She was another rather large lady, warm hearted, beautiful, all smiles and words of welcome. Wine and cakes were produced as they sat on her well-used sofa in her large splendid kitchen with polished copper pots and huge bunches of herbs hanging from the ceiling.

Her husband would return shortly and they could, of course have some chickens, she had so many chickens. They could have as many as they liked.

Arthur disappeared outside to see the dogs. The baby was good, sleeping on his mother's ample bosom and the little boy played with some kittens by the stove. Edward talked to the lovely Martha, all pink and round as a ripe peach. Ivy looked around considering what her life promised. This friendly kitchen with intoxicating smells, with cats snoozing by the range. Everywhere was a delight.

Ivy had always liked chickens, so left Edward and Martha chatting away to wander around the yard. She really had never seen so many different varieties before, all clucking away under the trees around the yard and in the fields beyond. She sat quietly watching them. They did not just look different, they had different characters too. It was not long before a fluffy golden chicken arrived on her lap, making wonderful clucking sounds. Ivy stroked its head. It was the first time she had ever stroked a chicken's head or, indeed, had one sitting on her lap, Ivy felt content. She certainly wanted to take this one home.

It was not long before the farmer, strong and able, returned. They could choose whatever they liked, so Ivy was left on her own to decide. She really wanted the golden fluffy one, also one or two of its sisters and a cockerel to form a trio. She also wanted the big black speckled ones, Morrans she thought they were called, she needed these, they would produce really large eggs for baking, and the black ones with fluffy legs were enchanting and of course Rhode Island reds which reminded her of her grandmother. "*Certainment, c'est possible tous est tres bien,*" agreed the farmer producing more boxes.

So with Arthur's enthusiastic help they set about chasing the chickens and filling their boxes. There were so many chickens, Ivy wanted them all.

Just as they were about to leave Martha came out proudly presenting Ivy with a present – a tiny cage in which was a very small rather plain brown bantam sitting on eight tiny eggs. This rather fierce bantam looked at Ivy and Ivy looked at the bantam. She did not like the look of her at all but she knew she could not refuse this rather doubtful present.

Arthur was insistent that Ivy and Edward follow him into a barn nearby. Inside the barn was dark after the bright sunlight outside, all they could see were golden eyes staring at them, then more, there were cats everywhere.

"*Chaque ferme au besoin de chat*," said the farmer, insisting that they take one. A large black cat with yellow eyes was passed over. The farmer said it was his best ratter.

"Oh dear! I had not thought about rats. I had not considered rats at all," muttered Ivy.

Next they followed Arthur into the back of the barn, to see a beautiful soft brown sheepdog with seven adorable puppies lying among heaps of straw. The puppies were only two weeks old. Arthur wanted to take them all home too. Ivy was very grateful that the puppies had to stay with their mother for at least five more weeks. She had five more weeks to settle into her new home before the arrival of another member of their growing household.

They left the farm joyfully after much hand-shaking and kissing, promising to return very soon. The truck was heavy now. The chickens squawked in the back as they manoeuvred over the rough track, the black cat was silent as it sat on Ivy's knee eyes staring, its claws outstretched.

It allowed itself to be calmed by Ivy's caresses and kind words – even if in a foreign language. They tried to be serious about where to put so many chickens, but they could not, they could not stop laughing.

Edward proposed emptying them all out together in the long barn. It seemed their only option so they travelled back to Les Vergers cheerful and ever hopeful. It seemed a very good idea. It was not long into the journey when Ivy became aware of hot liquid running down her leg. She did not move or indeed say anything. The fierce cat was frightened, it had relieved itself on her lap.

"Cat has never been in a car before," said a very wet and stinky Ivy. She continued caressing the cat, and when they arrived back at their farm she carried him gently into her kitchen making a cosy place for him by her beautiful black range, and buttered his paws. Cats love butter and washing off the butter would keep him occupied until he settled. Over in the yard, she found Arthur and Edward unloading the frightened chickens, all flapping and squawking, into the back barn. The men were having such fun among these crazy birds. Ivy left them to sort it, she really needed a shower. But no soap! However, with or without soap she was going to have some sort of shower. She stood naked in Edwards contraption completely relaxed, thinking it the most wonderful experience she had ever had, open to the elements with water pouring over her head.

Chapter 20
And so to Church

Ivy awoke. It was rather late. It appeared that Arthur had gone out early with Edward. Looking through the window she became aware that the usual hustle and bustle was not evident. This was Sunday. She went downstairs to eat something before venturing into the village. She found the two men unpacking the back of the 'heap' with bales of straw and sacks of grain. Of course, she had forgotten the chickens. No wonder she had slept so long, the day before had been a wonderful day, yet extremely tiring. Now there were so many small mouths to feed. Ivy ran down to the men, of course they were going to sort out the chickens. She wished she could help but she had made a commitment to the school-mistress, therefore to the whole village by now, to be at the 11 o'clock mass.

Ivy heard the church bells first, ringing out at least half an hour before the service was due. *This certainly gave people enough time to sort themselves out,* she thought.

She walked through the narrow streets with balconies overflowing with flowers, joining groups of people all hurrying in the same direction. The sound of the bells became louder across the mountains, her mountains! She realised that she was owning them already.

The priest, beautiful, resplendent in the morning sun, was waiting at the entrance right at the top of the church steps, greeting everyone as they arrived. Ivy felt so good to be there, the priest's greeting was so welcoming.

"There is an English sheet inside, waiting for you," he said quietly.

85

Inside it was cool, yet rather dark after her walk in the morning sun. Someone passed her the English translation sheet and she was shown to a special seat reserved for her right at the front. She would have preferred to sit at the back, but the pre-arranged seat had been carefully kept for her. They had made a point of acknowledging the new arrival from the big house.

All was quiet in the church. Ivy was so moved as she followed the Mass on her English sheet listening to a very young novice priest singing all the hymns in a high falsetto voice. He came forward to sing all the hymns by himself, his voice so clear and uplifting. No painful congregation here struggling with the high notes. The many people here were all coming together for an hour of friendship and love. This was not wasted on Ivy.

The mass ended, Ivy made her way out following the villagers, the children running ahead released from their imposed hour of reflection. She looked around noticing people chatting with an old lady caressing an equally old dog on her lap. Further on she saw a wrinkled old man seated with a scraggy sheepdog under his seat. Ivy noticed a great number of dogs. Would they have been welcomed in an English country church? She thought probably not. Here the old and the young were one. If they needed their doggy companions with them, it was accepted.

Coming out through the church door into the bright sunlight she saw the congregation making up for lost time, all talking at the top of their voices enquiring into each other's lives, showing off babies, gesticulating, smiling, kissing and hugging. The schoolmistress spied Ivy from a distance and started clapping. The whole congregation looked up, broke off their conversations joining in clapping vigorously. The children from the school rushed forward taking Ivy's hands dragging her into the midst of the crowd to meet their parents. The schoolmistress joined them translating. Ivy was overwhelmed with love for these warm joyful people. They continued their protestations of affection for another hour. And as she left them she realised that she was surrounded by children, all wanting to hold her hand. These were her children now.

Chapter 21
Cannes

It was hot, very hot as the early morning sun ushered in another day. All work on the farm had ceased. The village workers were helping out on the nearby farms. Farming here was a split second timing arrangement when all the villagers supported each other when help was needed harvesting crops. The new arrivals were quite happy needing a rest from all the excitements on the farm. They also needed light clothing. They decided to go on a trip to Cannes.

Cannes had a great harbour and was famous throughout the world for its beauty. They stood on an empty platform waiting for the train to travel down to the coast. Would it really arrive at this derelict place? When it did arrive it was a double decker. Ivy had never seen a double decker train before. They carefully climbed up the narrow stairs making their way to the front. They loved seeing the world from on high, the vineyards, orange and lemon trees and enormous exotic flowers growing on high branches.

By the time they reached Cannes, the train had stopped many times and was brimming with people all squeezed together like sardines all laughing and talking at the top of their voices.

Ivy absolutely loved the whole experience. It was so good being part of so many people of different nationalities. They left the train noticing that there were no barriers here or ticket inspectors on the train or platform. It had been like this in England when Ivy was a girl. She had gone to school with her sister on a steam train in the end compartment marked 'Ladies', with the guard in charge to make sure that they got off at the right station. What had happened to her England?

There were pavements and traffic on tarmac roads here. There were also carefully tended lawns and flower beds, so different from their village. They ambled down to the harbour, sat at an outside cafe and ordered drinks. There were boats, or were they called yachts? Anyway, they were the most amazing boats Ivy had ever seen, hundreds of them, huge boats with four or five decks all perfectly polished, and smaller editions all waiting, just waiting. But where were all the people? It was so quiet, the sky so blue, the sea so still, so incredibly beautiful in the gentle morning sun. The water glittered as if sprinkled with silver. They relaxed into the French way outside a cafe people watching.

Later, they moved on to the town and another cafe. Tiny handbag dogs were dragged along by tall elegant men. There were so many dogs, mostly tiny pedigree things. Ivy watched a particularly good-looking man sit down at a nearby table ordering a coffee. He placed his small dog, a Chihuahua, on his knee and proceeded to make love to it, almost as he would to a woman. He fondled it, kissed it on the mouth and between the ears. In return the little dog snuggled into his shoulder thoroughly licking his mouth, neck and shoulders. No one else seemed to be looking. It seemed to be the norm here, but it certainly would not have been the norm in Ivy's Exeter. And everyone looked so rich and wore such beautiful clothes.

Ivy separated from the men to go shopping alone, enjoying the freedom that all men and women need. She quickly found a charming shop selling really pretty cotton dresses and bikinis. *Pretty dresses preferably with sleeves would be lovely*, she thought. Was she too old for a bikini? With enthusiastic help from a leggy young girl she bought a really colourful confection in yellow and orange and a blue check dress that she could wear every day on the farm. She liked them both quite a lot, even if the more practical one in blue-check reminded her somewhat of her old school uniform. Then, on her way back to the cafe she fell in love with a pair of exquisite bronze strappy sandals, with heels. She had to have them. After that she restrained herself from looking into any other enticing shop windows. It was all so tempting.

Back in the cafe she sat alone, surrounded by her parcels and feeling a bit giggly. She felt so young. She smiled at the waiter ordering her first glass of Beaujolais.

She sipped it, really aware of how she felt, absorbing this new brave Ivy who dared to take a leap in the dark at an age when she was expected to lie down and wait for death! This was not her way now, it had not been her mother's way, who described an English seaside resort as being like an elephant's graveyard. Her mother had always been a 'live wire'. Why had it taken Ivy so long to realise her potential?

Edward and Arthur eventually returned with huge smiles on their faces, yet few parcels.

"We've had a wonderful time, looking at boats, buying shirts and, ah. I've bought a car!" said Edward. Ivy's eyes opened wide.

"Yes, we found it in an incredible place and it was such a good price I just could not leave it there. It's a real car, a proper car, also one that will cope with the rough tracks up to the farmhouse too."

Edward could not stop enthusing.

"What is it?" asked Ivy interrupting the flow of enthusiasm. "You will love it, Ma. It's a real peach of a car – a Mercedes convertible with two roofs. It's splendid and in perfect order. It's perfect."

"I love it, it's white with red leather seats and has a beautiful little steering-wheel," said Arthur.

"Very few miles on the clock. It's been owned by one man, a car fanatic, who has kept it locked up unused for years, a bargain." Edward stopped to take a breath.

"How will you like driving it on the wrong side of the road?" said Ivy, who could read her son perfectly and was not going to spoil his excitement by too many doubtful comments. He had had too many years being controlled by a stiff, self-indulgent wife. Ivy was glad that he had bought himself such a treat.

The new car was the only topic of conversation over lunch. Arthur was probably even more enthusiastic than his son. After all, he was the one who had found the man in the first place. The man had been sitting on a bench admiring the yachts when Arthur joined him while Edward had been organising their new clothes. So Arthur and his new friend, Harry, started talking about boats and cars and things. When Arthur said how much he loved cars it was arranged that he could go up to the man's house to look at his collection when Edward returned. They found themselves at a fabulous property adjoining the beach. In the beautifully maintained outhouses, all centrally heated were cars and more cars. They talked and talked. Edward so impressed Arthur's new friend, he was so enthusiastic and knowledgeable returning to one particular car again and again. "It's perfect," said Edward. "Would you like it?" asked Harry.

"You bet!" replied Edward. "So have it, I never use it now, such a pity. It's going cheap to you."

It did not take long for Edward to make up his mind, shaking hands with his new friend on the deal. Returning with Ivy sometime later they found that the car had been brought outside with Harry seated inside. "Come on, get in. We'll go for a spin," he called out. There was no hesitation. The two enthusiasts drove off in style into the hills beyond.

"What a place!" exclaimed Ivy.

Arthur showed her around as if it were his own, all the buildings, the gardens, boat house and jetty all in perfect order. "Such wealth for only one man!" ventured Ivy, waving her arms around.

Ivy and Arthur sat on the jetty, looking out to sea together all so beautiful and so still.

When Harry and Edward eventually returned in high spirits, a jubilant Edward was driving.

Arthur rushed over to the two men.

"How was it, Edward? Was it great? Did you just love driving it?"

Edward's huge smile said it all.

"Come on now, Edward, it's my turn," he cried out.

So Edward left with his father in the passenger seat, both thrilled to be in his new beautiful beast.

They were laughing exhilarated, all cares cast away.

It was arranged that Harry would deliver the Merc up to their farm in a couple of days.

Edward became very quiet, somewhat overwhelmed by his latest acquisition, as was Arthur, so it was left to Ivy to find out more about this intriguing man.

Chapter 22
Courage Is All

Monday arrived. Ivy, Edward and Arthur were awake early, eager to get up to the farm. The excitement of the previous day had certainly been overwhelming. The farm looked calm and beautiful in the early morning sunshine. Ivy hurried over to let the chickens out into the fresh air. She watched as they all rushed about in a frenzy digging holes, investigating their new surroundings. She threw them corn watching as they gathered around her feet. They seemed happy, separating into their little family groups. Ivy was intrigued, they were so territorial and the loud clucking of chickens reminded her of what they had taken on. She considered that they seemed much more refined than the human race. She loved them already.

Edward had found a perfect outhouse for his new car, but it was dank and dirty, for years a home for huge spiders and probably rats. Cobwebs obliterated the windows, mildew carpeted the floor, and an overwhelming acrid smell of past occupants pervaded. Could he really put his exquisite new car into this appalling place? Edward and Arthur decided to perform a miracle. It was going to be hot dirty work, a terrible job, but it had to be done.

Wearing their new shorts and old T-shirts, the two men moved in to start work. Ivy did not like spiders. She would concern herself with the living areas of the big newly painted barn, after all Sophie was coming at the end of the week. The village builders were working. Edward and Arthur were hopefully creating a fitting new home for the amazing car. Ivy looked at all the industry about her. She wanted to get the bedrooms sorted, but how? She just had to get down to the village, to make sure that the curtains would be ready, collect the provisions she had ordered and go to the market. It was market-day in the village, which meant she could buy everything there that she needed. She quickly realised that if she could arrange all this, they could actually move out of the *auberge* into their new home the following day. She walked over the yard, past 'the heap' to ask the men for help. They were completely involved in a thick haze of dust and detritus. She walked away, noticing that the car keys were still in place in the heap. She stopped and looked and looked again. Could she? Would she? She had not driven in years and certainly not on the wrong side of the road, with a steering wheel on the wrong side too. There was also a rocky mountain track with a precipice to carefully avoid. But Edward could do it and was now quite confident. Ivy climbed up into the driving seat, somehow pushed it forward and sitting up on an old coat left behind by someone or other, she felt rather pleased with herself. She turned on the engine, shaking somewhat, sitting awhile as she calmed herself down. Then courage. It was letting off the handbrake and putting the vehicle into gear. The vehicle lurched a bit, slowly moving forward around the yard. Several times she drove around the yard, avoiding chickens and the piles of builders' rubble until she felt sort of safe. But could she navigate the bends down to the village? She took a deep breath, quietly eased the heap away from the farm and onto the track. No one saw her, she was very grateful. She was going very, very slowly. She hoped she would not meet anyone on the way, backing was not a possibility. She held her breath.

Arriving in the village, now busy with people, she found a parking place on the edge. Somehow, she managed to stop and park rather professionally. She sat quietly, recovering from the driving ordeal, yet feeling rather proud of herself and 'the heap', which was not as terrifying as she had thought it would be. The sun was shining, the sky an incredible blue, the air filled with scents of flowers, all was so calm so beguiling. Ivy walked into the village really surprised at how many people she now knew who stopped to speak to her. She could say very little, her French was so poor, but she could smile, that seemed enough. This was a pretty self-sufficient village, where everyone seemed to know each other. They were all cheerful, really enjoying Market Day and introducing Ivy to their friends as if there was nothing to do in the world that was more important. An hour passed before Ivy was able to buy a thing, but she was enjoying herself feeling so alive and aware that she was really completely happy. She bought a couple of string bags for her shopping, all French people seemed to have string bags. The curtain lady waved from a distance, Ivy's curtains were ready. If Ivy would like to collect them, she would fix them in place that afternoon. Wonderful!

Ivy needed to do more shopping, household supplies, fruit and vegetables, a chicken, a dead chicken, which she wanted to cook on her lovely stove. No, she did not want a live chicken, she had many of those at home, nor a rabbit in a cage, she had them as pets as a child. She could not eat those. She was certainly not going to start eating rabbits now! She wanted bacon and sausages for breakfast, to accompany the eggs she felt sure they would find in the nesting boxes. And she wanted cheese, there were so many cheeses on display, fruit too, she wanted fruit. They would be growing their own fruit and vegetables soon.

Eventually, with a very heavy load Ivy arrived back at 'the heap'. Help arrived. A charming young man came to her aid lifting the heavy bags as if they were as light as thistledown. He wanted a lift up to her farm, he was looking for work. Ivy took a deep breath, not enjoying the thought of having a passenger, but agreed. She liked the look of this young man after all he had helped her. Starting on her slow journey up the mountain side, not daring to look down to her right, where a steep drop was waiting for the unwary, she said not a word until they arrived.

All was just as she had left, the chickens were still clucking, her son and husband were still hard at work among the spiders, while the builders were sitting under a tree sharing their lunch with each other. Nobody had missed her. The young man helped her out of 'the heap', carrying all her bags into the kitchen.

"*Vous êtes très charmante, très belle, merci beaucoup, madame,*" he said, then off he went to join the builders.

Ivy went into her beautiful kitchen which was cool and inviting. The larder was really cold, so the chicken, bacon, sausages, cheese butter, all would be fine, so would the fruit and vegetables. She was satisfied, reflecting that they really did not need a fridge here. The larder was magnificent with its slate shelves. She laid the table for a midday meal, added some wild flowers in a pot, and placed a carafe in the centre. She was becoming more French by the day. She called Edward and Arthur in, they had to be hungry! They were very hungry. They were also really, really filthy. And as they sat down in Ivy's immaculate kitchen, bits of straw and other nasties dropped off them. Ivy just smiled. They were so happy, unable to stop talking about what they were doing, and what was needed. Ivy, ever indulgent listened, watching them eat and eat. Nothing was left. They sat back completely satisfied and completely oblivious to the filthy droppings on Ivy's clean floor.

"We can move in tomorrow," Ivy said, casually.

"Can we? I'd love that," agreed Arthur.

"I think you are being a bit hopeful, Ma," said her sensible son.

"Yes, we can. The kitchen is stocked with enough food for a week. The curtain-lady is coming to fix up the curtains in the bedrooms this afternoon, and I am going to make up the beds. Tomorrow I plan to cook a celebration dinner," Ivy broke off, waiting for a reaction, but all was quiet. They were actually going to move in properly the next day.

"And actually, Edward, the heap is not so difficult to drive," she added. Edward was incredulous.

"You did not actually drive it," he spluttered,

"You really managed to get down to the village by yourself? You could have killed yourself."

"Well, I did. And, as you can see, I did not kill myself. I will never have to ask you to drive me again."

This Ivy, his mother, was a truly incredible woman.

Chapter 23
Moving-In Day

The farm was waiting for them, the newly organised garage was waiting for them, as yet no doors, but Edward, ever hopeful, had hitched up some of his plastic sheeting left over from Ivy's shower to cover the front. The curtains were up, the beds were made, and the chickens safely locked in. They piled all their few possessions into the back of the heap and with great charm and French expansiveness, they left the Auberge, promising to return very soon. Madame kissed them all and cried, her husband just kissed Ivy hugging the men expansively. It was all very moving. Ivy realised how much she owed these people, their kindness and their generosity had made their new world possible.

The move was remarkably simple. Edward had secured the help of Nicki the charming young man whom Ivy had driven up from the village. Between them they unpacked boxes, emptied 'the heap' and cleared the cobbled yard. Ivy packed away her clothes in her beautiful armoire and enjoyed sorting out both Arthur's and Edward's things. It seemed that there was a lot of washing to be done, really dirty washing. She could see her husband and son through the windows, making even more washing as they cleared the cobbled courtyard around the farm. She stood, fully absorbing her paradise.

There was no water as yet in the old laundry, so Ivy, ever imaginative, took the large pile of dirty washing to her outside shower and with a great deal of olive oil soap and surprisingly warm water heated by the sun, she plunged the lot into the old tin bath, poked it around with a stick and left it to soak. She did need a clothes-line, and she certainly needed help putting one up. Nicki happily obliged. She was very grateful that she had bought some pegs on that first day. Soon the washing was hanging on the line, the courtyard was cleared of builders' rubble, and everywhere was looking really good or 'shipshape' as they said in Devon. But the windows! They were opaque with so much filth clinging to them. Nicki found a hose from somewhere before joyously hosing down the windows. In fact, he hosed down the entire house and indeed himself, laughing hilariously all the time. It seemed that the water pressure was a power-force in itself coming down the mountain. Nicki was ever enthusiastic. Ivy drank the mountain water, she felt it tasted like the elixir of life. She looked up to the heavens above and said a huge 'Thank you,' as the sun shone down, and the gentle wind encompassed her with the perfumes of summer. Could anything surpass this? She sat quietly on the stone seat beside her kitchen door.

The black cat, her cat, wandered towards her. She put her hand down to stroke him, he jumped onto her knee purring a very loud purr. He liked it here too. She did not want this moment to pass, but men get hungry. She realised that the moment had passed. She needed to go to the kitchen. She loved her kitchen, the table with its odd chairs and wild flowers hanging from the ceiling. She loved her men, and she loved cooking. The cat followed her, she must give him a name, for the present he would have to be just 'CAT'.

Eventually the men had to stop work needing a shower after their day fighting off spiders and rats. It was Arthur, quickly followed by Edward who first tested Ivy's shower. She could hear the gong going nonstop accompanied by roars of laughter as she cooked her first real meal on the old range. The chicken bought from the village was roasting, vegetables were prepared, and a bowl of grapes and cheese sat on the side. It looked wonderful, smelt wonderful, and as she looked at 'CAT' she almost, but not quite purred. She went across the cobbled yard to shut in the chickens for the night, noting that they looked cosy and happy in their new surroundings. Ivy really liked her chickens, yet as she wandered back to her kitchen, she wondered how she could pet them one day, call them names, yet eat another the next. There was no understanding it.

Father, Son and Mother sat around the table, eating and drinking each other's health, congratulating themselves on the first day of their new life. The food was delicious, their home was not a dream, it was now reality. A great contentment enveloped them all and a cat looked on.

The next day Nicki arrived in navy dungarees and heavy working boots. He had a small parcel under his arm. "Pour interior chez nous," he said looking at Ivy.

It contained a clean white jacket.

Ivy knew she would need some help in the house. She liked Nicki, he was young, beautiful and so very helpful. He spoke no English, but he and Ivy seemed to understand each other, as if by telepathy. He had the dark swarthy features of the south, a big open smile, with dark-brown twinkly eyes. He was moderately tall, thin, too thin Ivy thought, she really must feed him up. He seemed to really value this lady. Young men were usually too busy enjoying their lives to take much interest in the elderly, but this young man was an exception. What she did not know was that after that first drive up the mountain-track he was full of admiration for this small, courageous English lady who could drive a truck up a mountain. Nicki proved invaluable, staying on day after day. He could turn his hand to anything, drains, plumbing, carpentry, and amazingly he was able to cook, helping Ivy in the kitchen. Indeed, Ivy soon discovered that his main forte was cooking.

He was able to chop vegetables so fast and expertly. He also was able to professionally deal with the fish and meat. He was far quicker than Ivy, and knew how to braise and grill to perfection, producing delicious meals, he had a real gift. *But he did not know how to make fruit cakes or pasties*, thought Ivy.

Chapter 24
Enter Harry

Harry arrived unexpectedly the next day, driving Edward's immaculate new car. It looked somewhat out of place in its new surroundings, but Harry did not care, in fact he was amazed by the natural unexpected beauty of this hidden gem. He wandered towards the only door which was open. Ivy was in her kitchen, she was cooking a typically English breakfast, bacon and eggs, sausages tomatoes with huge chunks of fried bread. The wonderful smell of fried bacon along with coffee was utterly inviting. Her men, Arthur and Edward, were hungry. Looking up she saw Harry standing there so polished, framed in the doorway. She also saw that he was almost, but not quite, handsome. He had to be about 65 and he was obviously very fit.

"It's late, we slept in, decided to miss breakfast have brunch, do join us," said Ivy smiling invitingly.

Harry looked at Ivy in her large stripy apron, hair pushed back, no make-up, smiling. Harry thought her quite beautiful. Harry really liked these generous people, so Harry enjoyed a second breakfast accompanied by many anecdotes and lots of marmalade.

They knew the car was special, but it had not sunk in how special. Edward could not wait to inspect it again, he just stood there looking at this beautiful beast. Arthur was certainly even more excited than usual looking at the dashboard, touching the stumpy gear stick and the fine leather on the steering wheel. Ivy watched quietly, it felt so good to see her son and husband so completely happy together, Harry too. Eventually Harry left father and son together looking for Ivy, he really wanted to see more of the farmhouse. They walked together looking over the outbuildings and the expansive gardens. Colourful chickens happily ran around and fierce black cat watched from behind a disused shed. They looked at the ancient grapevines on the terraces, the ripe figs and the old olive trees. All was so good. They watched as the enthusiastic builders repaired steps and worked on the terraces. The atmosphere was of enormous energy and excitement as one thing after another came to life. Ivy felt so blessed, feeling rather proud of their achievements so far. Harry was full of good ideas, finding it easy to talk to this very special lady.

"Before I retired to France, I developed a large engineering business in Birmingham, living outside in the country with many acres. It was pretty derelict when I bought it. Not unlike this. I saw its potential, and quickly restored it." As he looked around, he realised that these people had the same work-ethic that he had. He also realised that he missed the excitement of developing a project with his wife, who had always been there to back him up. He felt a great wave of loss. It had been three years since his wife's death and he realised that he had done nothing much since, not even going to see old friends. He had felt so traumatised that in many ways he felt paralysed, somehow numb, disconnected, at least that was until Arthur had started talking to him on that bench as he stared past the yachts into the distance.

Harry had been a solitary boy, his father had died for his country in a brutal battle he was told. His gentle mother had not really recovered. So he had taken over the responsible manly position in the house. It was usual then, not now, he thought. He went to a grammar school, was bright but left early to work in a garage to support his mother, then took on a second job to support himself and bought a motorbike. How he loved that bike, taking it to the Isle of Man for the TT races. Such thrills. Then he acquired an old Ford truck to do deliveries and things, met Maria when she was only seventeen, instantly falling in love. Her beauty, her quiet energy reminded him of his mother. Anyway, Maria quickly got pregnant and they married. Her parents were not too pleased, but as his business developed and children arrived, they forgave his lack of family or connections. He now realised that he had not appreciated Maria enough. His whole interest had been his work and developing his business which just grew and grew.

And as it grew the time he spent with his wife and family became less. He was sorry for that, so much time wasted. Then he had an affair, couldn't even remember her name now, and something in his relationship with his wife was lost. They continued rubbing along, staying together until her death. This big, powerful man was really surprised by the pain he felt by her passing.

The three men, Harry, Edward and Arthur, were like three excited schoolboys discussing the new car and garage then it was off to find materials. Ivy was left with Nicki who was busy repairing the outside terrace. She liked having Nicki around, who seemed to sense everything she needed. He came into the kitchen, he had found an old vine lying on the ground at the end of the terrace, its wooden supports rotted away. He took Ivy by the hand to see. When Nicki returned, he was very dirty but obviously very pleased with himself. He stood watching Ivy baking, she had flour in her hair on her nose just about everywhere and as she worked, she sang completely oblivious of this short, dark young man gazing at her in awe.

He quietly cleaned himself up under the outside tap, returning to the kitchen immaculate in his starched white cotton jacket. Ivy looked up. How could this young man transform himself so quickly? She had noticed how clean and smart most of the French looked on Sundays, even in this rustic hill-top village. He came over to the table where she stood, chopping up carrots and taking the knife from her hand and began chopping in a completely quick professional way. Where did he come from, and what was his background? Ivy could see that he loved cooking as much as she did. The pair really enjoyed working together, this extraordinary English lady with wispy white hair and this gorgeous young man touched by the sun.

The men returned in two trucks. Edward in one, a rather disagreeable man in the other. He looked sleazy and unsmiling. He made his way towards Edward's garage carrying an armful of wires and a toolbox. It seemed that Harry felt that they really needed electricity in the garage. This man was an electrician of some repute. He was also going to organise lighting throughout the farmhouse. Ivy was delighted, she would have electric light instead of candles although she did love candles in the evening. Edward was also delighted, as he could now use the power tools Harry had bought.

Nicki looked worried and would not go near their latest helper. He did not like him at all. Neither did Arthur, who kept his distance spending his time communing with the chickens. Ivy could sense that something was wrong. She waited until she found Edward alone.

"Your man, the electrician, I do not like him at all, neither does Nicki or indeed Arthur. Arthur at this moment is sitting with the chickens and won't come in. I do feel rather worried. What can we do?"

Edward was concerned, he loved his mother and knew she would not complain unless she felt it serious. He went off to find Nicki, who was about to leave.

"*Doucement, Nicki, vous avez un problème?*" He put his arm around the young man's shoulders.

"*Il faut que j'y aille. J'n le aime pas cette homme. Il n'es pas bien.*" Nicky would say no more but was adamant about leaving.

"*Returnez bientot, il passez depuis quatre jours,*" Edward called after him.

He went to look in at the chicken house. Where was his father? He heard him first, singing a little song to his favourite chicken in the gloom. He was seated on an upturned bail of straw, hugging his knees. He was not happy, "Come on in, Dad, it's late and there is a delicious meal waiting for us," enthused Edward.

Arthur looked doubtful.

"Where's that man? I do not like him."

"He's gone," said Edward, taking his father's arm. Together they walked towards the kitchen, where they were met by lovely homely smells and Ivy's sweet smiles. They forgot the disturbance of the worrying electrician, but he was not to be forgotten.

Chapter 25
Beautiful Machines

Ivy and Arthur took off for a day out together, Ivy driving 'the heap'. She felt quite confident now, but still uncomfortable on some of the tortuous bends. Someone above had to be looking after her.

They found themselves in a small town they had not been to before, setting out to investigate on foot. Ivy realised that she had not spent much time alone with Arthur since collecting him from the nursing home. So much had happened since. It seemed so long ago. She realised that both she and Arthur had changed, both developing into the different people they were now. They say that you can't change after 70, thought Ivy, but they were wrong whoever 'they' were.

The town was larger than their village, much noisier, more cars and more motorbikes. Ivy was grateful that she had parked on the edge of town. They walked past smart shops, holding hands like teenagers inspired by so much urban activity. They found a good little restaurant on the side of a square overlooking a rather beautiful church shaded by trees. It reminded Ivy in some ways of the little French restaurant in Exeter overlooking the cathedral green they had enjoyed in their other life. They sat together people-watching, drinking coffee and nibbling biscuits. They watched a group of young men leaning on their motorbikes, smiling, chatting, gesticulating and smoking. They were all smoking. They were young, nothing was going to stop them. Arthur left her to look at the machines, somehow chatting away to the young men. His broken French was hilarious and they loved him for it, showing off their own expertise in English.

To Ivy's surprise, she watched her husband get onto the back of the most enormous black motorbike, then to her horror saw him roar off into the distance behind a very wild young man clutching him from behind. She left her seat, rushing outside waving wildly at the group of young men. "Help. Help. Where has my husband gone? My husband, where is he? Where has he gone?" Ivy was distraught. "*Doucement, doucement, madame. Tout est bien, il reviendra,*" they replied smiling.

Ivy stood on the pavement, helpless. She had to trust them. In time the enormous black motorbike returned, Arthur on the back completely exhilarated.

"*Bravo! Bravo grande pere!*" shouted the youths, standing, waving, all hugging each other including Ivy.

They quickly made friends all getting together in the outside cafe, practising their English with Arthur and Ivy who enjoyed practicing their French-speak. At length the party left on foot with Ivy and Arthur in their midst, going they knew not where.

They arrived at a sort of warehouse full of bikes, motorbikes of every description. Ivy had never seen so many in one place. Arthur wanted one, sitting on one after another, handling the shiny controls with glee. The young men were having a great time with this crazy old man. But Ivy was not that interested in motorbikes, she was more intrigued by an ancient piano covered in a blanket pushed back into a corner. She pulled back the blanket opening it up. She played a few notes, the sound was exceptional but the piano was dusty and certainly out of tune. She shook her head, this piano certainly deserved better.

In time a shabby old man in a black boiler-suit came over to her with an old brown dog trailing behind. The boys called him 'grande pere'. *He spoke heavily accented English rather well,* Ivy thought.

"I used to play a lot when I was young but no more. My family have taken over this place. The young do not like pianos; they only like motorbikes," he said.

"That's dreadful. I used to play a very long time ago. I have not played in years but I love to hear a piano being played," sympathised Ivy.

"The boys say the piano is in the way and looks a mess. They want it gone, but it is my only memory of ze times past," said the old man mournfully.

"You must not let it go. It's beautiful. We can house it for you in our place up in the mountains. We will love it, look after it, then you can come up and play it whenever you like," said Ivy spontaneously.

Grand pere could hardly believe what he was hearing. Of course it could go to a new home up in the mountains with this beautiful lady. In fact he would like to go up in the mountains with this beautiful lady.

"The boys could bring it up in a couple of days. I vill come and tune it and you can play it too."

Ivy smiled a smile of total recognition. She had found another friend.

Quietly they went over to reclaim Arthur from his new friends with their beautiful machines. He did not want to leave. Only when they promised to come up with the piano very soon would he agree.

But what about the dog? Ivy had seen one of the boys kick it away from under his feet. She watched as it limped away. The old man was shaking his head, but what could he do? "We can't leave it here, dogs and motor bikes don't mix," said the always compassionate Ivy.

"Zis is no home for a dog or a piano," uttered the old man quietly.

"Would you like us to give him a proper home where he will be looked after and loved too?" Ivy asked gently.

"Zat would be wonderful," the old man paused, thinking on. "Ee deserves better than this. Zis is no place for a dog." The old man spoke to the old dog trying to explain why he could not keep him anymore.

He handed him over to Arthur and walked away. The old dog lay silent on the floor of the heap, he seemed to understand.

"You can come up whenever you like to see him, any time you want, you can take him back," Ivy called after him.

Arthur was delighted, he loved dogs and had missed Scruffy a lot when Hellene took him back to Devon.

On returning home, Ivy could see there was light in the ever-improving garage and her kitchen too. She was very tired, it had been an eventful day. She thought her driving was really rather good now and she liked Edward's truck. She mused about the piano. Where would they put it? Would it really arrive before long? Arthur thought only about motorbikes while caressing the old brown dog's ears. The table was laid for a meal and lovely smells emanated from her old black range. Cat was purring a loud contented purr. Nicki was back, proudly wearing his immaculate white jacket. He stood there ready to serve a wonderful meal that he had cooked while they were away. Ivy was so pleased to see him, running up to him hugging him French style.

"Oh, Nicki, Nicki, I am so pleased to see you. I thought you had gone," she cried.

Nicki smiled a huge smile.

Arthur took the old dog into the barn behind the chickens settling him down in the straw. It was cosy there. He left to collect food and water for him. When he returned, he noticed that the dog had not moved, his eyes said it all. Arthur stayed with him.

The men worked into the night on the garage. They had organised a curious sleeping arrangement. Edward shared his twin-bedded room with Harry, they had made a sort of dog's bed in the corner if Arthur wanted to join them. They knew he would not want to miss any of the male speak. When all was quiet, he slipped into Ivy's bed.

Chapter 26
Things Fall into Place

The following morning it was rather windy, and as Ivy slipped across to her shower, she realised that it was really not good enough for Sophie, who was used to Parisian comfort. An open shower and box-loo was amusing for a while but it was far from comfortable. The men did not seem to mind the rustic conditions, the garage was much more important to them, but for a smart Parisian lady? Sophie was due in a few days, somehow they had to have a bathroom. Ivy's first approach was to Harry, as she knew that both Edward and Arthur had become car fanatics overnight, the garage was becoming larger and larger, a bathroom was really not their priority.

"Yes, you are right, of course we cannot expect a Parisian lady to make do with the present arrangements. I'll see what can be done," said Harry.

He made his way to the builders on the terraces, soon returning with a cheerful group of men who seemed to know exactly what was needed. Harry discussed with the enthusiastic workers all possibilities. They decided to build a completely new structure at the end of the barn, under the existing roof. The structure would have two new bathrooms, one off Ivy's room and one off the spare where Sophie was to sleep. The space underneath they would think about another day. The men seemed to like the present shower arrangements, so it was agreed that they could keep using them. Ivy was delighted, she could see it all happening in front of her eyes.

Edward decided to help the builders, he wanted to be sure that all the windows were being put in the right place! There seemed to be no planning applications in this part of France, he mused – so much easier – after all he was only doing interior repairs and the men seemed to know what they were doing. Arthur decided to leave the garage for a bit. He wanted to stay with the old dog. He also wanted to help Nicki in the kitchen. He liked cooking, he liked Nicki, and he really liked 'Cat', who seemed to like him too. They would sit together by Ivy's warm range with Arthur talking to fierce cat in a strange mixture of schoolboy French and English. Fierce Cat purred fiercely. His real fierceness quickly disappeared when Arthur was around, and the old brown dog lay peacefully outside.

Ivy and Harry got into Edward's truck and made off down the hill, with Ivy driving. Ivy was glad Harry did not suggest taking the wheel, she was really proud of her newly acquired skill. She particularly liked swinging the beast around the dangerous corners somehow avoiding the worst rocks in the way. Harry just smiled and said nothing. He was enjoying himself and was looking forward to Ivy's reaction to his favourite place.

They arrived at a sort of warehouse set back from the road. It was as dilapidated as the village garage, but without a fierce chained dog. This place was completely disorganised with an assortment of sinks, baths and bidets lying about on the ground and covered in dirt, while customers wandered around at will – no assistance here. This reclamation yard enchanted Ivy. She was intrigued by it all, feeling as Edward had on seeing the cars in Harrys garage. She wanted everything. With Harry's help she contained her enthusiasm. She chose two splendid baths with brass fitments and attached showers hanging down from ornate pendulums. Pretty washbasins and loos, hand painted with delicate flowers were next, followed by two glass mirrors the size of her old garage doors in Exeter. But would they fit in the new bathrooms, and would the floor take the weight? Harry assured her that all would be well. If necessary, they could put in an RSJ – whatever that was. She was glad that Edward had organised wide openings for the doors and windows. They arranged for it all to be delivered the following day and Ivy, ever hopeful, laid any doubts to rest. She felt that her purchases were a bargain and was really thrilled, Ivy liked a bargain. Few people wanted ancient bathrooms nowadays, but she did, she felt very good indeed. She really liked Harry, he was thoughtful, kind and humorous. He had sort of become an unofficial guest who was beginning to feel part of the family. But he had a fabulous home of his own. When was he going back there? He showed no sign of leaving.

"Would you like me to drive? There's just one other place I want to show you," suggested Harry.

Realising that she was pretty tired, Ivy agreed, grateful not to be at the wheel. They arrived at another old yard, this one was even more disorganised than the last, littered with planks of wood, carved lintels, doors, spiral staircases and large, really large, marble fireplaces and there were tables and chairs, armoires of every size and many chests, everything so exotic. She would come back with Edward another day. It was really amazing, it planted so many ideas in her head, she wanted to share her ideas with her son.

On their return to the farm, the outside shells of the new bathrooms were up, the first layer of plaster was waiting to be applied. There were great discussions about weight-bearing going on. Ivy had chosen really heavy things. She was never going to have a small plastic bath again. As she listened she began to appreciate all the work involved in developing their dream, from Edward's open shower and bath which she had loved, to the dramatic washing emporiums, one of which was to be her own truly luxurious bathroom.

The men worked on the bathrooms tirelessly. The outside terraces would have to wait. Water was pumped over from their own well, icy and fresh. A proper tank and boiler were fitted and a R.S.J. to be on the safe side. The solid wooden floors were sound and would look wonderful once polished. There would also be hot water and electricity. And there would be water, plenty of water. All would be finished in time for Sophie's arrival.

Edward Arthur and Harry worked with the builders on the polishing of floors while Ivy cleaned windows and polished chairs.

When it was all finished, they crowded into Ivy's kitchen where a great deal of wine was drunk and fruit cake eaten as they sprawled around the table congratulating themselves on their splendid feat.

Chapter 27
And the Nightingales Sang

With the bathroom finished, and a proper lavatory, Ivy felt relaxed about Sophie coming to stay. She was due the following day but had rung to say she would be a little late. A young friend had offered her a lift. Ivy was looking forward to Sophie coming but was happy to have a little more time to really sort things out. Nicki proved very helpful, cleaning windows, sweeping up, even repairing the structure of the outside terrace, which included pruning and fixing the old vines in place. It would be a perfect place to sit facing the sun shaded by the vines. Ivy realised that they needed another table. Everyone would want to sit in this wonderful outside space. The kitchen table was far too heavy to move. She had no idea where to get one. That afternoon she had arranged to see the schoolmistress again. She realised that she could not really begin teaching the children until after Sophie had left. She walked slowly down the track, now well-used, to the village below, still marvelling as she looked around inhaling the scents of herbs and flowers. Bird-song rang out, crickets tickerty ticked and bees buzzed. Ivy continued to absorb her new heaven. She would never tire of all this.

The schoolmistress welcomed her into her cosy cottage, making her welcome with tea and squashed fly biscuits. Ivy had not had one of these since she was a child. They sat on her charming terrace with bright red geraniums covering every available space. They chatted easily.

Ivy explained that she could not come down to teach the children for a while, but would welcome them up at the farm. They both agreed that this would be a splendid idea, particularly in the summer. The children would love it. Ivy had to admit that she had no suitable table for them to work on. The only table she possessed was in the kitchen and was much too heavy to move outside for the children. "Oh do not concern yourself, I have a big old trestle table at the back of the schoolroom which is never used. You can have that. It's not too heavy you can collect it any time." The trestle table would be perfect.

Ivy returned later with Nicki, who manhandled the school table into the back of the heap. He might look small but he was strong, thought Ivy. The table fitted the terrace perfectly. They agreed they would bring out the kitchen chairs when necessary.

It was not long before Edward, Arthur and Harry arrived in the kitchen in need of a drink. They quickly carried out the kitchen chairs, relaxing with a bottle of deliciously cold wine. Ivy and Nicki were congratulated on the new terrace, they really liked sitting there. Nicki beamed with pleasure. Ivy just smiled, her happiness almost palpable.

It was not long before the Priest arrived with Monsieur and Madame from the *auberge*. Monsieur's big truck was piled high with furniture, wooden pews, and several chairs that were no longer needed by the church. They thought that Ivy would like them for the children. She certainly would, but so many!

Ivy had plenty of food in the larder, Monsieur found several bottles of wine secreted behind his driving seat and Madame proudly brought forth a huge apple and apricot tart.

The Priest said a blessing. What a feast they had! It was twilight when they all drifted away, leaving behind only the throbbing of nightingales on the evening air. They had forgotten the disturbing man who had put in the electrics and who had frightened both Arthur and Nicki at the time.

Chapter 28
Freedom

It was a quiet day the day before Sophie was due to arrive with no builders in evidence. Edward and Harry were still at it transforming the garage. Arthur stayed around the farm, old brown dog always at his feet now. Ivy decided to have a quiet day, stay in bed late then take a long bath in her amazing bathroom.

She really appreciated the luxurious soaking in the warm water aware that all her aches and pains quickly disappeared. Then she looked at herself in that huge wonderful mirror, gilded and decorated with birds. The mirror told all. She looked and looked again, carefully for the first time since leaving Paris. She saw that she had certainly muscled-up, her face was more relaxed and smiley, but she could also see it was really dry, more lined, certainly needing cream, and lots of it. Her hair looked bad too, really bad, so sad after Hellen's expert cut when it had looked so good. Now it was all straggly again. She had to do something about it. She must go down to the town below where she knew there had to be a good hairdresser. So hopping into the truck she drove off.

"Back soon," she called out.

Such freedom! Such liberty was hers for the taking.

Finding herself in the town below her village she looked around for a hairdresser. She could not let herself down, with Sophie's imminent arrival.

She quickly became aware that several very smart ladies were going in or coming out of one particular establishment. This had to be the one. Ivy walked in.

"Yes, someone could do it now," said the exquisite receptionist, in perfect English.

Ivy found herself seated in front of an ornate mirror, with a beautiful young girl feeling her hair.

"*Vous cheveaux sont enviables.*"

Ivy lay back as her hair was washed and washed again, then her head was massaged and massaged again. All these young assistants were so kind and so attentive. Ivy pondered on her youth and the ravages of time. Such a short time. She was going to enjoy every moment of what was left to her. The stylist took a very long time trimming then re-trimming her hair, concentrating on every little snip with her very sharp scissors. Ivy felt totally indulged, pampered even.

"*Bien, tres tres bien, Vous êtes vraiment belle,*" said the assistant with some satisfaction.

Ivy looked in the mirror. She could only agree. This haircut, this sensational haircut, had transformed the neglected country-woman into another person entirely.

Into the bustling street she walked, with her head held high, her step lighter.

A chemist's shop was nearby. There were so many chemists in this town, there seemed to be a chemists on every street corner. She needed a great deal of cream to fight off the ravages of time. She bought two huge pots hoping for the best.

Sitting down in a cafe nearby she smiled at the world around her, sipping coffee and chatting happily to Monsieur the proprietor in her ever-improving schoolgirl French. He certainly understood her.

She then walked into a small boutique, bought a wonderful scarf, an incredibly pretty white blouse in finely pleated lawn with handmade buttonholes and an exquisite leather belt.

Hellen had really shown her how to shop in Paris. Ivy found herself enjoying engaging with the clever young assistant who seemed to know instinctively what would suit her. Women really need to be pampered a bit. Ivy understood that the men in her life had always been too involved in their own projects to remember this, so she bought the lovely creations, pleasurably watching as they were carefully packed in lots of soft tissue paper.

On arriving back at the farm, she quickly took her purchases up to her bedroom. She felt rather guilty, she had bought so little for herself in the past. She unpacked the neatly folded items, from the beautiful carrier bag. She could not wait to try the blouse on again, with her mother's lovely fine grey skirt cut on the cross which moved as she walked, and the gold strappy sandals. She walked into her bathroom to look at herself again in the mirror, that enormous mirror. It told another story. She looked good, felt good, almost renewed. She walked across to her kitchen with pride. Nicki had done so much while she was away, now there was not a thing out of place. Even the table on the terrace had a clean cloth on it, with a bowl of flowers in the centre.

"A place for everything, and everything in its place" was her father's mantra, and this was certainly the case with Nicki.

All was still as she wandered around to the garage to find the men. So many changes had been made to both the farm and herself, she thought.

Hearing the laughter from the pit under Edward's new car, Ivy called out.

They heard her voice, saw her legs, and came up for air. "Wow!" cried Harry. "You look amazing. We must go out to celebrate. We have just finished the garage."

Ivy looked at the men, they were so filthy, with so much oil on their hands, in their hair, on everything. Their clothes were certainly beyond repair. The garage, its benches, its tools, were immaculate, all organised onto shelves or into boxes under the benches. She knew they could not be kept away from their project for long, but they wanted to go out to celebrate, not just finishing the garage but also Ivy's new persona. The men thoroughly washed, showering outside in Ivy's old shower, but Edward, naughty Edward showered in her new bathroom that he had said he did not want!

"Well, they will have to have a good basic shower-room downstairs, or my new very special bathroom will be no more," whispered Ivy to herself. Edward's shower had served its purpose. Some proper workmen's overalls are needed too, and soon."

The three clean but rather dishevelled men and Ivy roared down the mountainside all squeezed into Edward's heap. They arrived at Harry's rather grand home throwing themselves into the huge comfortable armchairs. Harry opened a bottle of Vivre Clique and then another.

"Wonderful, I love Champagne," said Ivy quietly.

They were then ushered from this designer drawing-room into another white designer dining-room that overlooked manicured lawns to the sea beyond. Raul Duffy paintings hung on the walls. A long mahogany table was set with highly polished silver and glass. Blue and white Spode china stood on the sideboard. Wonderful smells emanated from the kitchen.

How could Harry stay away from this magnificent place for so long? wondered Ivy.

He had been sort of camping with them for more than a week.

Utterly delicious food arrived, course after course, carried in by an elegant upright man-servant, resplendent in white starched jacket. So this was how it was done in posh French houses. Nicki, her Nicki, must have picked it up somewhere, but where? Ivy was glad that she was wearing her new super-fine white blouse, her mother's pale grey skirt, and of course her very pretty gold sandals. She was very pleased that the hairdresser had done such a good job that day, and she was thankful that she did not disgrace this beautiful dining room.

They left Harry after this truly memorable evening, feeling somewhat sad, as they had all grown fond of this really strange man of secrets.

Chapter 29
Could It Really Happen?

The shock when they arrived back at the farmhouse was tangible. All the lights were on, illuminating the whole courtyard. All was silent, strangely the old brown dog was silent too. The new garage doors were swinging on their hinges his beautiful car gone.

Edward raced to the empty garage. The car had really gone, the tools too. He could not believe his eyes, all their work was trashed.

But where was the old brown dog? Arthur raced off to look for him, he would be in his favourite place among the straw bales. This time old brown dog did not come out to meet him. Arthur looked around. He found him at last. Old brown dog lay dead at his feet his head bashed in. Arthur screamed, he could not stop screaming, a deep primeval scream.

Edward came running, then Ivy. They dragged this distraught man away from the horror of the night. With arms around him they somehow got him into Ivy's kitchen. Shocked, they all drank quantities of sweet tea by the range. They could say very little. Black cat jumped onto Arthur's knee.

In the morning, Edward knew what he had to do. He collected a spade from the shed, walked to the end of Arthurs' vineyard and dug a very large hole. Returning to the house he found a rather worn yet lovely blanket, wrapped the body of old brown dog in it and waited for his mother and father to join him. It was a beautiful spot overlooking the valley. All was still in the early morning, they picked flowers from the hillside throwing them over the carefully placed body. Then they covered him with soil, made a cross with twigs, said a prayer and left. Arthur was still holding on to old brown dog's collar. But it would not bring him back.

Down in the village Edward found the mayor. Someone must know something, it was obviously planned. The village was soon talking of nothing else. Who could have done such a wicked thing? Edward rang Harry who was back at the farm waiting for him on his return.

"It had to have been taken in a large removal van. The wide tire tracks tell it all," said Harry seriously.

He was soon on the phone contacting friends who would know about such shady dealings. They all seemed to owe Harry favours. His very presence calmed everything down. "Thank heavens you're here Harry," said Ivy with feeling.

It was not long before Harry received a short phone call, they had to move fast.

"Come on Edward I think they have found it."

Edward carefully picked up the dog collar from the table where Arthur had left it, he could not leave it behind.

The two men left in Harry's car, driving at speed down the treacherous track to the village then on to the town below.

They were very serious.

They arrived outside a disused warehouse where Harry's reluctant friends were waiting.

"It's inside. Watch it, they're pretty nasty."

Harry and Edward did not wait to hear any more. They crept through a side door into a disused body shop. They saw Edwards's car up on a ramp, the number plate already removed.

Edward's stunning red car was about to turn green. A mechanic of some sort was already holding a spray gun in his hand.

Edward was much stronger than this poor looking man. Grabbing him from behind by the collar he began shaking him unmercifully. Harry grabbed Edwards arm.

"Enough Edward, enough, I think he's had enough." Edward looked as if he was capable of murder. Harry thought he probably was. The small pallid man obviously thought so too.

Harry spoke.

"Who put you up to this? You'd better talk, or my friend will surely throttle you."

The frightened man tried to wriggle free, but Edward had him in a firm grip. He was certainly not leaving this creep with his car.

"Well," said Harry menacingly. "The boss. Where is he?"

"Back soon," gasped the man.

"Edward, lose the poor devil, he's had enough," repeated Harry.

Edward and Harry waited. Who was the boss? Was he dangerous? Harry certainly thought so as he fingered the gun he had secreted in his inside pocket. He kept it only for emergencies now. He thought this was an emergency.

Time slipped by, the three men not moving. What had they got themselves into?

A shriek of brakes, tires scraping on gravel was the first they heard, then the banging of car doors followed by two men hotly arguing. Harry and Edward listened. They were certainly arguing about the car.

"When will it be ready? Is it okay?" one demanded.

This man was wild and noisy, the other as sleek as a cat.

They could see the men through a cracked window. Still loudly arguing they came through the double doors. They saw Harry and Edward immediately, also the pitiful man in Edward's grip.

They stared at their visitors both tall strong and very much in control. The sleek man with cat-like appearance was the first to speak.

"Want to buy this nice little goer? Needs a new spray, ready next week," he said.

"No, we do not," replied Harry calmly, keeping the fury out of his voice.

"We just want to drive it away, just as it is. And of course, we want the old number plates, and the soft top too."

"What makes you think you can do that?" hissed the wild-looking one.

Harry had not spent his life cosseted from this type of world. He took out his gun and began quietly fingering it. They watched.

"It's time for us to leave and we're not going without the car." Harry sounded menacing, "Get it together and we're off. If you want trouble, you will get it."

Harry and his gun were impressive. No more was said. The garage doors were opened. The car rolled out and the number plates thrown in the back.

Edward walked towards his car deep in thought, then abruptly stopped.

Taking old brown dog's collar from his pocket he looked directly at his adversary. Then he powerfully hurled it straight into his face.

"This is from old brown dog," he cried and drove away leaving a shrieking bleeding man behind.

Harry and his gun watched.

"Now get the soft top into the back of my car. You know who I am, and I don't forget."

They did not hesitate.

Harry drove off grinning. It had been a satisfactory day.

The return of Edward's car was something of a miracle. Everyone in the village had been really upset. Nothing like it had ever happened before. Posies of flowers, cheeses, small puddings and pies were all delivered to Ivy's kitchen door. They were so kind.

It was not long before it was understood that the seedy electrician that Arthur and Nicki had disliked was the culprit. His loose words in the Auberge had started it all off. His doubtful friends took it from there.

It was not long before the chicken couple from the other side of the mountain arrived, having heard the shocking news.

They had bought them a present. Monsieur reached into the back of his truck bringing out first one puppy, a gorgeous puppy, and then another. Arthur was ecstatic.

It was wonderful to see these all-embracing people again. The two puppies ran around the courtyard with Arthur in hot pursuit. He was traumatised by the brutal attack on old brown dog, so it was good to see him playing with the puppies.

Ivy took their friends onto the terrace where they enjoyed eating another apricot tart, drinking wine and catching up.

The baby was well, the boy growing, chickens increasing, the harvest coming along nicely and the tomatoes ready for chutney. It was all so simple, so real. And as the puppies played outside painful memories were put aside.

Chapter 30
An Undignified Entrance

It all happened at once. So much noise intruded on the perfect peace of the early morning. Screeching motorbikes and young men, followed by an ancient camper-van with an old man. The piano was making an undignified entrance.

Ivy was thrilled to see the piano, but where to put it? The young men wanted to manhandle it into an outside shed, but Ivy had other ideas, as did the old man. The main house was not just big, it was really extraordinarily big. The empty salon looked enormous when empty, something the size of a tennis-court Ivy thought. She had not played tennis for many years, she could be wrong of course. But as she looked, really looked at the neglected room for the first time she could see what a truly splendid room it was, with panelled walls and a huge stone fireplace. She could see that its beauty had been almost obliterated but not quite. The relentless mistrals of the winter had done their worst, but the room remained intact. Anyway, the piano was going in there, it deserved to be there. Ivy considered that the room deserved the piano. It must have had a piano in the past. It was a room for entertaining. She could almost see, in the depths of her imagination, people dancing to the strains of music around her. There had to have been love there too, she could feel it, she sighed with pleasure.

Her reveries were interrupted by the old man.

"We 'av to clean zi place up before we can put my piano in here. We have lots of strong young men, we must use them."

Ivy agreed.

Enthusiastically, they all set about cleaning up the years of accumulated filth.

They removed the ivy from the windows and manhandled the tree growing through the floor. Cleaning the fireplace was a mammoth task. Birds had nested in the chimney for many years past, throwing down twigs and feathers which seemed to be stuck together with a sort of concrete which was certainly not man-made. And so much soot, black sticky soot covered much of the floor.

A lot can be done in a few hours with power behind the broom.

The young men, accompanied by Arthur, Edward and Nicki, made a great game of working, amid shrieks of laughter. Ivy and the old man looked on mesmerised.

Eventually the piano was graciously delivered into its new home. They were all so pleased, congratulating each other profusely.

Edward loved the piano, but could not wait to show off his new toy to the lads.

"This is great, now come with me I can't wait to show you my amazing new car."

"Bring it out," they all cried.

Edward brought it out into the courtyard the sunlight shone on its gleaming bodywork. It really did look amazing. They wanted to look at it properly, they wanted to sit in it, look under the bonnet, go for a spin.

They could hear a low rumbling before it appeared, an immaculate long black machine, with open top, and carrying two equally immaculate looking passengers. It was sleek sexy with dramatic lines – a Porsche, the best Porsche money could buy. They all gathered around this wonderful new shining beast. It was being driven by an equally stunning young man, both elegant and smiley. And as he went around to disengage his passenger, Ivy realised that it was Sophie. They hugged and kissed and wept. They had missed each other so much.

Leaving the excited men all involved in the intricacies of cars, heads under the bonnet, legs stuck out from under the wheels, others trying out the leather seating and gazing at the instruments. The two ladies walked away, arm in arm. The piano forgotten, the cars forgotten, friendship was all.

Edward and Arthur and Francois of the Porsche, and the young men of the motorbikes were all completely involved with the cars.

"How fast did they go?" was repeated and repeated. The old man looked on with an amused smile.

Into this hubbub Harry arrived, resplendent in another fabulous car – a Jaguar XK120 this time. He had missed them all so decided to take his baby for a spin. The boys were thrilled to see another great car. Harry could scarcely get out as willing hands tried to pull him up from the very low-slung driving seat. All were asking questions without waiting for answers. He got out laughing, he did not want to talk cars, he wanted to talk to Ivy. He saw her with Sophie in the old rose garden, so taking the car keys he left the boys with Edward and Francois joining the ladies the garden.

Ivy quickly realised that the elegant young man, Sophie's friend, was the same young man she had met in the Paris tea shop behind the Notre Dame. And she remembered that he had called her beautiful. Was Francois going to be part of their life?

The motor bikers left promising to return, but the old man stayed, not wanting to leave his treasured piano.

And Harry stayed, not wanting to leave his friends for an empty house on the beach. And Sophie's friend Francois also stayed. He really liked these people, the surroundings and more than anything, he loved the old man's piano. "Does it work?" he enquired.

"*Vraiment*. I 'av played it all my life, 'ere, there, everywhere," he replied.

"We are just giving it a home for the time being," added Ivy. The old man removed the dust-sheet with a flourish, revealing a gleaming gem of a piano, a Steinway. He had spent the last few days cleaning polishing and tuning it. All were completely amazed. The old man sat down quietly on the piano stool, adjusted it, waited a little, then played. They all listened in awe. When he finished, he just stood up adjusting his old working clothes as if adjusting a dinner jacket. There was silence, then they all began clapping and clapping. "Bravo, bravo, old man," they shouted.

"Wonderful, so very wonderful," whispered Ivy.

She found herself weeping with joy, this old man was a maestro.

Overwhelmed with emotion they tracked down the path to the Auberge, a time to recover was needed. It had been an unforgettable experience. Phillippi, the old man, was in a state of shock, he had not played his piano seriously for years, only tuning it from time to time. He had thought he was just a useless old man. But as he played, he realised that he was not useless, he was a pianist, one who had played in concert halls all around Europe, and he could still play! It took some absorbing. He still had something to offer. Here in this beautiful place people recognised his gifts. He felt very, very grateful.

It was quite late when they left the Auberge. Beauty surrounded them as they walked through the seemingly empty village. What a night! Poetry was in the air. They could hear only the sound of their echoing footfalls. Only a scurry of cats and a door banging in the distance.

Suddenly Ivy remembered the chickens. They had completely forgotten the chickens. They had not shut them up. Edward and Arthur raced up the track, followed rather more slowly by Harry, Ivy, Sophie and the old man all enveloped in their memories in this gentle night.

Edward was waiting for them outside the farm, the chickens were safe.

"We must get a proper dog quickly. The new puppies were barking when we returned, but they are not really guard dogs,"

"The old brown dog would have kept the foxes away," whispered Phillippi. Then he ambled off alone to his empty camper van for the night.

It was late, so Harry stayed sharing Edward's bedroom and as before, Arthur crept in beside Ivy. Sophie enjoyed her delightful room with opulent bathroom. Francois had to put up with the small daybed on the landing. It was not ideal, but it was late and they were all tired.

Francois had not had a good night, he decided to go for a walkabout early the next morning. He alone was awake needing to stretch his legs. The daybed was really too short for a man of his height! Hanging his legs over the end was not his idea of comfort. He walked down the track to the village. Although early, the village was coming to life. He could see the industry inside the houses, people preparing breakfasts gearing up for the day, others were already outside tending their gardens. He noticed one old woman dashing down to a small hut at the bottom of her garden with a newspaper under her arm and it was not for reading! He smiled, he understood these people. He could hear them calling to their neighbours across the street. He could hear the cocks crowing, hens cackling, doors slamming and shutters opening. Church bells were ringing out, echoing throughout the streets and the church clock chimed in the distance. Even the birds knew it was time to wake up and sing. Francois wanted to sing. He saw that the boulangerie was open, the smell of freshly baked bread was irresistible. He chatted away with monsieur, bought several baguettes and croissants still hot from the oven then made his way back up to the farm, overwhelmed by a feeling of utter contentment.

At the farmhouse Ivy and Sophie were bustling around the kitchen, coffee was already on the go.

He really loved it here, so different from the constant moving of being part of a well-known group of musicians in a world of competition and wild parties.

He had been travelling for years. Now was a time for peace and stability. Two smiling ladies welcomed him with love and coffee. What more could a man want?

Arthur arrived with a basket of eggs. He loved opening up the chickens in the morning and collecting their eggs. He knew that the chickens liked him as much as he liked them. He was teaching them English and knew that they understood him!

Then the old man Phillippi arrived with a very large packet of bacon, so they scrambled eggs, fried bacon and ate the baguettes with lots of Sophie's homemade marmalade.

Ivy wanted to show Sophie and Phillippi around.
Could they really make a garden here?

They looked at the exhausted terraces, the gnarled olive trees, the carpets of wild flowers, the waterfall cascading down through the rocks, the neglected vineyard. They were incredulous.

"How did you find this little Eden?" they both asked.

Ivy still felt the same way about it as she had on first seeing it. She thanked God every day. It was not difficult to thank God in this peaceful place.

"It will not take long to make the garden, it looks poor now but the soil is very good," offered Phillippi.

"And there are many roses here already, they only need pruning," added Sophie.

"The vegetable garden just needs digging over.

You could be self-sufficient in no time," they both agreed.

Sophie and Phillippi were deep in conversation discussing the gardens. They both knew so much.

Ivy was no great gardener so she left them. She could hear music coming from the salon of the main house, and it was not the piano. All the windows and doors were thrown open. In the doorway, looking magnificent was Francois completely involved in music. He was making his clarinet sing. Ivy loved the sound of a clarinet, it reminded her of her father who used to play alongside the radio when she was a child. She sat on the step outside quietly listening. It was wonderful. Then she heard voices singing, this time a sort of male harmony. Who was it? She got up. It was Edward and Harry. She had forgotten that Edward could sing, and Harry too. It was really beautiful. She was thrilled and amazed. It seemed that the men had more in common than cars.

Chapter 31
Not Enough Beds!

Edward and Arthur were in the garage as usual. Sophie sat quietly in the garden just absorbing the beauty which surrounded her. She loved it here and wanted to share it with her niece. She picked up the phone.

Hellene answered, she was just leaving for the South of France with her old friend Sue.

"I can't wait to see you again and of course Ivy and Arthur. We will bring Scruffy and be with you by the end of the week. Goodbye, darling Sophie."

"Wonderful, really wonderful dearest, I can't wait to see you again."

What a brief conversation. Dear Sophie was given no time to share any news but was really thrilled at the prospect of seeing her favourite niece. The young are so busy now, they have so little time to listen, she reflected. She remembered being much the same when she was young. But where could they stay? Scruffy too.

She looked for Ivy who was on the outside terrace, sitting calmly with her phone to her ear.

"Yes, yes, of course," she heard her friend say enthusiastically.

"Goodbye."

"Tony, my eldest son with his sons and Edward's sons are all driving down to visit. It's really wonderful but where can we put them all?"

"Hellen and her friend Sue are driving down at this moment too, also Scruffy. Where can we put them?" added Sophie. The two ladies fell about laughing. It was so good that all these young friends and relations were descending on them, but where could they put them all?

They sat on the terrace in the gentle morning sun quietly considering how best to house all these very welcome guests. One thing was certain, Arthur would be overjoyed to see Scruffy again.

It was decided that the girls would have to stay at the Auberge and walk up every day. Tony would share Edward's room and the boys, teenage boys (there were four of them) would have to camp in the garden. They would like that. So it was settled.

A trip down to the town in 'the heap' provided all the necessary camping equipment and more food, a considerable amount of food. Boys of that age eat so much!

Ivy and Sophie returned from the village having talked to Monsieur and Madame at the Auberge. Monsieur and Madame were really pleased to see them. Ivy realised that she felt completely at home with these kind people. Nothing seemed to be a problem for them. They had helped them overcome so many obstacles at the farm. They would be friends for life. So they all sat together, relaxing under the now-familiar olive tree, sipping wine and exchanging news. Of course they would have the girls to stay.

Back at the farm all was peaceful as they lingered over a delicious meal. The heat of the midday sun and a delicious meal left everyone feeling very sleepy in this quiet heaven, but it was not long before they could see Phillippi driving up the track in his old camper van, this time followed by a large open truck, overflowing with small trees.

"A friend's nursery was closing down so I bought the lot for a song." He was so pleased with himself. "There are so many different varieties of apples. We can have an apple orchard."

"You are so clever Phillippi," the ladies chorused.

Each tree was placed just where Phillippi indicated, with Edward and Arthur digging hole after hole and the ladies filling in with compost. Soon, very soon, an orchard appeared.

It was late, very late, it had been really strenuous work, they were tired, yet Phillippi could not wait to spring another surprise. His camper van was packed with roses, pinks and lavender. The evening light quietly eroded all further endeavours, so happily they ambled back to Ivy's kitchen to recover. A huge steaming dish was waiting for them on the table and wine glasses just waiting to be filled. Nikki had performed a miracle.

The next day Phillippi's lads arrived on their great black machines. They were really enthusiastic and strong. Sophie and Phillippi sorted out all the plants and in no time a rose garden appeared as out of nowhere interspersed with pinks and lavender. It looked marvellous and it had not taken long with so much help from the boys. Grandpere was really delighted with his boys and could not stop hugging them.

The following day all was still. Phillippi had left in his dilapidated camper van and Harry had returned to his house on the beach. Sophie had also left early to discuss music with Francois. The builders had gone off to help out on another farm.

It was late afternoon when they arrived, Tony in his huge Range Rover with a gaggle of excited noisy young men hanging out of the windows. The family fell about hugging each other, all talking at the tops of their voices.

"It looks great. In fact, it all looks fantastic," broke in Tony looking around.

The cat was snoozing on the terrace and the two puppies were playing around Ivy's feet. He looked at the farmhouse, the size and beauty of it all. His boys would say he was 'gobsmacked'.

"How did you do it?" he gasped.

Edward had no intention of going into all that, he had more thrilling things to show his brother, dragging him off to the garage.

"Come on, Tone, something special to show you."

He grabbed his brother by the arm taking him across the courtyard.

Flinging open the wide doors of his garage he revealed his prize possession.

"There, isn't she a beauty, and all mine. I can hardly believe it."

Tony was astounded. How could his quiet unostentatious brother own such a marvellous machine? He had very mixed feelings. His young brother, his less-able brother, had all this! A fabulous sports car too. Edward's sons and nephews were equally impressed and soon Edward became aware of a creeping feeling of respect which was developing in them. He realised that he had always deferred to his older more dominant brother, then had carried on deferring to his controlling wife, then later on his children. Now, in his new life, he was not deferring to anyone. The change was absolute. He had taken a leap in the dark and it felt good.

Ivy loved having her boys and their boys around but was exhausted by the emotion of it all, so she slipped away to her beautiful bedroom for a bit of peace, noting how important it was to have a pause even when overwhelmed with happiness. Later Sophie returned from visiting Francois. She needed a pause from the beautiful Francois and his friends, noting that she needed space when surrounded by so many young men for any length of time.

The young band were a noisy colourful group thrilled to be staying in a great big house in the south of France, but Sophie, dear Sophie needed the quiet companionship of her friend Ivy, who was waiting for her at the farmhouse.

They walked together quietly through the gardens absorbing all the sounds and sights which filtered through the air. Women, these women, needed space to think and feel, away from the strong dominance of men. They knew they loved and valued men, but they also knew that they were a different species. The sexes were very different, how they ever managed to intertwine was a question they left open.

Chapter 32
Ideas and Implications

While quietly eating a picnic lunch the following day, sitting on a bank of wild flowers beneath the big olive tree our extended family fell into talking about what they could do to remain in this enchanting place. No one wanted to leave – ever.

"First of all, we have to make ourselves self-sufficient. If we all work together we could make it happen," said the old man seriously.

"We could certainly turn out great food," said Ivy and Sophie together.

"This place is magic – and we could do play readings." Sophie had been an actress.

"And I could put on concerts. We could play our hearts out here," added Francois.

"I could put on concerts too, and I could teach, giving great master classes up here," said Phillippi.

"It would be good to do something which involves the whole village," suggested Ivy.

"I can do planning and of course Harry is a financial wizard," added Edward.

"And so we shall have a music festival," suggested Ivy. So a music festival was born.

The first thing Francois did was to go back to his house in the village to talk to his group. Would they like to be involved in this new project? His group were thrilled to be asked. Time in the south of France with the lovely Francois was not to be turned down.

The first thing Edward did was talk to his brother Tony to run ideas past him. Tony was always a good sounding-board.

He agreed it had some mileage. So Edward went down to the village to talk to his friends the builders. They were really happy to do more work for this affable Englishman.

Harry readily agreed to head up the financial side. He could hardly wait to get started.

Phillippi drove down to the town below to collect his sons. Some serious manual labour was needed to transform the gardens into an area suitable for outside events. The cobbled courtyard was certainly large enough for big events but it needed a great deal of work.

Ivy and Sophie, with Nicky's help, could organise a small restaurant. The kitchen was certainly big enough. It was all very exciting.

Arthur, dear Arthur, wanted to make the vineyard his own, and make wine to supply the restaurant, and indeed the entire village.

Wonderful activity was all.

Edward came back from the village rather pleased with what he had achieved. The workers were able to start the following Monday. This would give him time to absorb all that a music festival would have on their peaceful lives. He worked on drawings.

Harry left quietly in his beloved car, completely aware of the financial sorting out that had to be done.

Francois left, returning with his clarinet, a trumpet and a saxophone. He played them all by turn, his notes echoing around the mountainside. As Ivy listened she realised that there would be time, time for everyone.

Arthur was pacing out the vineyard, not seeing it as it was but as it would be, flourishing and fruitful. He was so very happy, ending up in the chicken enclosure, sitting on a bale of straw telling his favourite chicken all about his plans. Strange, how these French chickens understood his every word!

Together Ivy and Sophie prepared the evening meal, becoming reflective. Were they taking on too much? But what else had life to offer these two elderly ladies? And, of course they had to consider Arthur, with his dementia progressing. They looked their world in the eye, embracing it. They were both strong, resilient women who knew about love.

The following evening found the small family and friends quiet, wondering about their new venture.

"Do we really dare?" whispered Ivy.

She recalled her time in the Church of St Julian le Pauvre in Paris. She remembered her prayers, they were so simple then. Now it was quite different, she had been given so much more.

Sophie remembered her bleak life after her husband died, the years of emptiness before Ivy and Arthur came into it. "Of course we dare," she said firmly looking at her friend. It was Arthur who broke the silence of the table. He wanted to be sociable, have fun, he did not like or understand this change of mood.

"I'm going down to the Auberge," he said.

"I'm coming, too. I'll show you my new house," added Francois. Edward and Tony could not resist a visit to Francois's house, so the four men departed, leaving Ivy and Sophie sitting together on the terrace as the sun receded, the dusk arriving so slowly that they hardly noticed. They sat in companionable silence, aware only of their commitment to each other, and their extraordinary bond.

Edward, Arthur and Tony returned. The ladies could hear them well before they arrived, their laughter and noisy repartee broke into their world.

"Francois's house is huge, really huge," said Arthur.

"No garden, but a great roof terrace overlooking the entire village," added Edward.

"We shared a bottle of wine then another talking over ideas for the music festival."

"It is such a great idea," added Tony.

They could not stop congratulating themselves on 'their' idea. The ladies just smiled.

The young men, Ivy's grandchildren, were having a great time organising and reorganising their tents away from the main house. Ivy could hear them from the kitchen where she and Sophie were happily cooking. The young loved splashing around in the icy mountain water as it rushed down over the rocks into a small deep pool beneath them. The brave ones dropped their bumbags and jumped in, coming out spluttering and shocked by the icy water.

The others raced around shouting encouragement. Thank heavens for Nicki who arrived at 7 o'clock sharp, working energetically clearing up and assisting wherever he was needed; He seemed to be needed everywhere, the gardens needed watering day and night, the kitchen and terrace needed washing down every day and the boys were always needing help with their tents which were constantly falling apart.

"It is not a good thing to anchor them on a rock face," suggested Phillippi.

They liked the tents where they had put them and were not going to move them. Nicki laughed, enjoying the company of the young.

Edward and Tony worked alongside the builders realising the value of these stalwart men. The brothers were constantly in need of plasters and had many bruises on their hands, feet and legs. They did not complain, it was really good to spend time in each other's company in the open air with the sun on their backs.

They decided to take everyone out for a meal. They all deserved something special.

"Ask Harry, he always knows the best places," said Edward.

"Chez Henri is the best fish restaurant on the coast," Harry said without hesitation.

Chapter 33
Chez Henri

The ladies were told to wear their best and the young told to scrub up as they were going out somewhere special. They would drive down to the coast in a convoy. Edward and Tony would lead in Edward's Merc. followed by Ivy and Sophie in the heap. Phillippi, Arthur and the grandchildren would form the rear guard in the camper van. The puppies would be left behind with Nicki, who had agreed to guard the farm. As yet the puppies were too wild to take out and could not be relied upon to deter foxes.

All in all, it promised to be a very good evening.

Harry was waiting with Francois outside Chez Henri when they arrived. The restaurant was really, really smart.

Harry had booked the special long table overlooking the sea.

As they walked in, Ivy noted the white linen tablecloths and napkins, the polished silver, the shining glasses and the waiters standing erect with large white napkins folded over their arms. So many flowers stood in huge glass containers around them, and beautiful pictures hung on the walls.

This was not casual French but the most formal of formal. How would Arthur and the young react?

Harry, ever considerate, had ordered a set menu in advance. He wanted them to experience the best of French food without the difficulties of sorting out a menu. He knew Tony wanted to pick up the bill, but he insisted that the drinks were on him. With this agreed they sat down to wait.

Wonderful Champagne cocktails arrived first in exquisite glasses with absolutely delicious herring pate on toast on the side. Then several waiters came forth carrying enormous silver platters piled high with seafood which they majestically placed on the silver stands on the centre of the table. Crested plates were sitting in front of them waiting to be filled and implements suggestive of a hospital operating theatre sat on the side. The boys had no idea what to do with them. It was pure theatre.

There were large prawns, tiny shrimps, enormous oysters mussels and scallops all in their shells. This was topped with huge wild looking lobsters. It looked amazing, almost daunting. Could they really eat all this and how?

Large empty bowls had been placed in front of them. Harry and Tony cheerfully gave out instructions. The boys could not wait to dive in pulling the prawns apart and aiming the carcasses into the waiting bowls. They were so excited some went in others missed, so much laughter, such glorious fun.

Arthur waxed lyrical over the oysters, he had completely forgotten how much he loved them, eating his way through eight. Phillippi had also forgotten how he had enjoyed good shellfish in the past. These two elderly men just gorged, smiling at each other in complete satisfaction.

Harry had ordered delicious French wines to compliment it all. He had a permanent smile on his face as he watched the hilarity played out around him.

Everyone was enjoying themselves so much that they scarcely noticed the evening sun lowering itself into the silver sparkling water below.

Eventually, about an hour or so later, when the empty shells had been taken away and the tablecloths changed, they sat waiting for what was to come next. Could they really eat anymore?

It arrived on an enormous silver platter carried aloft by an incredibly strong waiter his muscles rippling with the effort. The largest sea bass that Ivy had ever seen had arrived. "It has to be over a metre long," chorused the boys.

Ivy and Sophie could smell aubergines, onions and ginger, and herbs, wonderful exotic herbs. This was the work of an accomplished artist.

The young whooped with excitement as large pieces of the fish were expertly carved and placed in front of them. Everyone felt like whooping. Another hour passed as they ate their way through this feast, not even noticing that the world outside had descended into darkness.

A pudding followed, some sort of lemon posset and a chocolate mousse which Ivy loved. Then thick dark sweet coffee. All so memorable and so delicious.

It was late when they left the restaurant, they had been there nearly three hours, yet they had hardly noticed the time pass. It was quite dark and the air cool. They could hear the gentle ebb of the waves on the breakwater. No other sound, everywhere still.

Ivy felt weary, could she really drive all the way back to the farm in the heap?

Harry as ever came to the rescue.

"The ladies cannot possibly drive back at this time of night, I will drive them back. Edward can collect the heap in the morning."

The convoy back to the farm found Harry leading the way with the ladies comfortably settled in the back of his Daimler. Edward followed one of his sons beside him backed up by Phillippi's camper van with a gaggle of young men singing their heads off. Francois and Tony followed sedately in his beautiful black Porsche.

The crescent moon with a scattering of brilliant stars lit their way, an owl hooted and foxes scattered. They avoided the holes and precipices getting around the fallen rocks and switchback corners, even managing to stay clear of a small deer munching at the side of the road. Ivy and Sophie slept, happy to be driven back to the farm by Harry.

Chapter 34
Not a Good Idea

Ivy left early, she wanted to see her friends from the other side of the mountain. Their chickens gave her such pleasure as well as so many eggs. She had grown attached to the small brown bantam with fierce eyes who was still patiently sitting on her eight tiny eggs. She remembered how long her own pregnancy had lasted and the patience she had had to endure in those last weeks.

It was an overcast day, not the sublime sunlight and clear blue sky she had become used to. Nevertheless, she was pleased, as she knew the journey would be quite long so welcomed the cooler weather. She waved goodbye to everyone and left driving the heap, stopping to pick up the puppies on the way. As yet the puppies had no names. She had grown very fond of them and she liked having them around? They seemed very pleased to be with her following her everywhere. "Did they know she was visiting their mother this time?" She remembered the journey well from the last time they went there. The heap was full of empty boxes then. They had left with 34 chickens, a sitting bantam, and a large black cat which sat on Ivy's knee. She really had not wanted the bantam or the cat, now she loved them both. She also loved those crazy puppies sitting behind her. She had no problems now driving on the right hand side of the road, avoiding potholes.

Now she felt capable and in control, but she was not in control of the weather.

The sky turned from grey to black. Heavy bursts of rain began to fall followed by violent claps of thunder, brilliant streaks of lightening traced across the sky. Ivy pulled off the track, she did not like this at all. The puppies were frightened, whining and cosying up to her for comfort.

"It's all right, it will pass," she repeated as she hugged them. But the storm did not pass, it became more violent throwing everything it had in Ivy's direction. She had never experienced a storm like this in England. This was a deluge and she had little protection from it. She stopped, pulling into the side of the track.

After an hour or so, Ivy had lost count of the time. She decided to turn around and make her way back home, but the track was a river, a wild torrent of water. Ivy could scarcely see. She pulled the heap over underneath an overhanging rock. It got worse. Ivy felt frightened and alone, very alone.

Why had she left in the heap to go up the mountains in such uncertain whether? She knew she had courage, but she also knew she could be foolhardy. This was certainly not a good idea. Edward had warned her, but she had not listened to him.

She began to feel very ashamed of herself as she looked into the soulful eyes of the puppies. Of course they needed to pee. Somehow, they got out of the truck, the wind doing its best to knock them over. Ivy held onto the side of the heap only aware of the deafening noise and water pouring down her neck and back.

Many hours passed. It was getting dark, Ivy decided to try again, hoping that the heap was as strong as it looked. The wind was still raging and the rain continued to pound down upon her. The heap juddered down the track slivering from side to side, now more like a river. Somehow, she guided it around the bends and boulders, keeping her very real fear in check. She would allow herself to be afraid when she returned to safety. She realised that she had driven a long way when she saw a small farm somewhere in the distance. Where was she? She knew that she was truly lost.

She had to get out of the heap into the raging storm to reach the farm. She needed help. Somehow, she made her way over the rough unwieldy ground on foot as she stumbled over stones in the mud grazing her knees and filling her shoes with water.

The farm was further than she expected. She began to feel very weak. A door of a nearby barn opened before her. A short round man grabbed her by the arms dragging her in out of the deluge.

It was a relief to be out of the rain, but she quickly realised that she was surrounded by men, about forty of them. What was going to happen? They looked pleasant enough. One of them would surely speak English. She tried to speak, first in English then in her completely inadequate French. No one understood her. What was she to do? She felt nervous. The round man, her saviour, took control.

He sat her down firmly on a nearby bench thrusting a most enormous sausage into her hands. It had to be 18 inches long. Ivy was so hungry. She found herself greedily stuffing it into her mouth. Yes, yes, she would like another.

"*Merci, merci beaucoup, le deux si vous plais,*" she managed to say.

The man thrust two more into her hands.

"*Pour les chiens,*" stammered Ivy. She managed a smile. He then passed her a great mug of beer, then a huge slice of apple tart. Nothing had tasted more delicious.

She began to feel better. Her fear abated as she looked around at the smiling faces surrounding her. These were kind people. All these wonderful Frenchmen, who could not speak a word of English, made her welcome, fed her and watered her, then drew a rudimentary map for her of the area.

How did they know where she lived?

Returning to the heap, rain still lashing down Ivy gave the sausages to the puppies. They were as grateful as she had been. She was smiling as she watched them. She was no longer fearful, she had a map.

At last she found herself on the right track back to the farm, her farm, her home. The storm abated and the sun came out.

A thoughtful Ivy drove back quite slowly determined to be mindful of the weather in future. She had learnt that the sun did not always shine in the south of France.

Family and friends had been distressed by her thoughtless actions, and she was not going to let that happen again.

Chapter 35
Problems, More Problems

Everything seemed to be moving very fast! Edward and Tony wandered out to inspect the proposed areas for the concert. The salon was certainly large enough for quite big concerts. The double doors all along one side opening onto the courtyard let in an enormous amount of light. It would be perfectly possible to accommodate at least 200 people. But how to seat them? And where would they put cars and other transport? It seemed an impossible problem.

They wandered around the outbuildings and gardens feeling utterly disheartened. There had to be a way, but what, and how?

They hardly spoke. The chickens clucked, the cat sat purring in the sun, the women tended the roses. The old man hoed the vegetables and the young men and Arthur were joyfully working on the vineyard.

Edward and Tony felt impotent.

Much later after another picnic lunch where all of the workers shared in the general excitement the two men remained silent. Ivy and Sophie were aware that something was wrong, but were also aware that it was not a time to question. They returned to their roses.

Two large furniture vans could be seen climbing up the hill towards the village. Harry was leading the way in his favourite X.K. They all stopped to watch. Was it really coming up to the farm?

"It is coming here," they shouted.

Harry and the furniture van pulled up in the courtyard. "What is it, Harry?" cried Arthur.

"I think there is a problem," added Ivy.

Harry looked around the joyful faces of all the workers, becoming aware of the quiet concern of Edward and Tony. What was their problem? He did not ask.

"Come and see what I have picked up at the reclamation yard. They had just dismantled an old cinema," he said enthusiastically.

When the back of the first van was opened, they could see row upon row of red plush seating from another era. "Wonderful," they all gasped.

The unbelievable seating was quickly unloaded. There were so many seats; altogether far too many. The contents of the second van were unloaded onto the courtyard. "What are we going to do with them all?" queried Ivy.

"Expand!" shouted Edward re-energised.

"And there are so many empty houses in the village we can acquire," added Francois.

"But what about the parking of cars," said Tony prosaically?

"There is a huge old garage at the end of the village. We can park cars there and get a bus to ferry people up the hill," said Harry, inspired. Into this group the colourful gang of young men arrived carrying a great many musical instruments and singing at the top of their voices.

"Come on, we've a readymade concert venue here," cried Francois. They followed him into the salon. The musicians couldn't wait to climb onto the makeshift stage with Phillippi sitting in front of his piano. Spontaneous music echoed across Les Vergers to the village and across the mountains.

Ivy sat on the plush seating with Arthur holding her hand. She was feeling incredibly blessed. She had taken a leap in the dark and dared. She had dared to break free from the restrictions of old age and moved onto another life filled with people, music, love and laughter. She knew it would not be easy, she knew she would have to face the real problems of her husband's progressive disease, but she had close friends now, and her family around. She was not alone.

With so many people staying, the ladies became fully occupied with feeding them all, it was down to the village every day for food. The men were working enthusiastically with the builders the first-aid tin was always at the ready. The garden continued to develop apace with Phillippi in charge, his lads doing the manual work. Arthur's vineyard was developing too, with help from an expert wine growing neighbour. Music could be heard echoing across the mountains. Francois and his group could not stop playing.

Into this menage of activity, Hellen and Sue arrived in Sue's small Fiat car overflowing with boxes and Scruffy. These two gorgeous women stunned them all, one tall and fair with enormous blue eyes, the other, shall we say, utterly beautiful with an angelic smile.

The men young and old quickly gathered around. Edward made introductions calling to his mother and Sophie to see who had arrived. Scruffy quickly found Arthur. What a riotous reunion they had, with Scruffy jumping all over Arthur licking around his ears, indeed everywhere. Edward had forgotten how he was attracted to Hellene and Hellene could not believe that this tall bronzed man was the same stiff Englishman she had met at Aunt Sophie's house in Paris.

That evening they all went down to the Auberge where they feasted talking over each other and hugging and kissing French style. Talk centred around the music festival, Hellen and Sue quickly becoming involved.

Sue had retired early from teaching French at a large school in Stratford upon Avon. She had put on many plays with her students. She could also sing. François was particularly thrilled.

"We need you, we really need you," he said with meaning. Sue felt wanted and appreciated, their eye contact said it all.

Hellene was so thrilled to be with her Aunt Sophie that she hardly noticed Edward quietly gazing at her.

Chapter 36
Phillippi Finds Himself

Phillippi arrived early at the kitchen door looking rather splendid, he had shaved and tidied himself up.

"I'm just going down to the village on business," he said casually, and left.

The ladies looked at each other in amazement. "What does he mean?" said Ivy.

"I don't know, but he looks years younger now he's got rid of those awful whiskers," replied Sophie.

Phillippi arrived at the Mayor's establishment much as Edward had done only a couple of months before.

No, he did not want to rent a small cottage, he wanted to buy a proper house with history, a garden too. He wanted to live there permanently and yes he wanted to die there. The Mayor was puzzled. Why did this strange man want to buy a house in this remote village? He gave him a list of places available. Phillippi left with just one. He only wanted to look at one.

He walked slowly through the village which was not yet fully awake, he walked past the church, the bells peeling the hour, then on and up another track overgrown with vegetation.

All of a sudden, he saw it, recognised it, an elegant stone house partially hidden behind a high stone wall, the gates swinging on rusty hinges. The garden was overgrown, yet he could see that in the past it had been spectacular.

He looked at this lovely old house with the hills and valleys in the distance.

He acknowledged that this house was to be his house. It was perfect. It was elegant and spacious, the gardens a delight.

He had to live there he had been living in the camper van for far too long.

"This is my home," he called out to the universe and to a mongrel dog that was sitting at the gate.

On returning to the Mayor's office he was told that this wonderful house was immediately available.

He shook hands with the mayor, an agreement was signed on the spot and he left a secret smile playing all over his face.

The Mayor was a very happy man. He had sold two large houses and let another all in a few weeks. He shut shop, making his way to his favourite cafe to down a couple of brandies.

Phillippi felt really pleased with himself, but he was uncertain how his new friends would feel about having him as a permanent neighbour. They were delighted when he told them, yet somewhat surprised. They had underestimated this old man. Ivy and Sophie wanted to be taken to see it immediately. Phillippi just smiled and smiled. He could not stop smiling.

"Of course I shall need a dog. I have missed my old brown dog, now I am ready for a new one," he said somewhat tentatively.

"I have somehow acquired a sort of stray from the village. It followed me around as I looked over the house and garden. I will have that dog, he would love to live there, and the garden would be perfect for both of us."

The gardens at Les Vergers were his love and he loved all the people who lived there, but he wanted and needed a home of his own now and he wanted that dog. He returned to the house to look for him. The dog was waiting by the gate.

When Phillippi arrived back at Les Vergers, Harry had arrived. He was surrounded by Edward and the builders pouring over plans on the terrace. They were very excited. Lovely Nicki was in attendance, wearing his smart white jacket and producing endless food and drink. So, it was really going to happen! The music festival became more of a reality by the minute.

He looked around, he could see so much activity on the slopes. Arthur, the lads and Scruffy were working away on the vines. Phillippi's lads seemed to know exactly what to do and Arthur loved directing them, throwing his arms around and shouting directions that only scruffy dog seemed to understand. Ivy could see that Arthur might yet have his dream of a vineyard and make wine for everyone.

Phillippi left the men, joining Ivy and Sophie somewhat relieved to leave the serious planning to others. He preferred feminine company anyway and he preferred being creative outside. It was not long before he got out ropes and sticks laying out plans for the music festival gardens.

It was going to be quite an undertaking. It would have to be amazing with water features, streams and rills. There was no stopping now.

Sophie and Phillippi knew a great deal about gardens.

Ivy knew a great deal about cooking and what was essential to her. Mint was essential, she missed mint. Lemons were essential too, so they would have lemon trees. She could hardly wait to pick her own lemons.

They were called back to the house. The three men had put away their plans and were sitting with Arthur and the boys. A decision had been made. They were all going down to Harrys place for a barbecue.

They drove down in a convoy again, two elegant sports cars, Tony's range rover, the heap, the camper van and seven very loud and very powerful black motorbikes. All the vehicles roared down the mountainside with shouting, singing and laughter. Harrys house could not fail to impress. The boys for once were quiet as they walked around. The barbecue was already set up and waiting for them.

They were hot, very hot. They could see the sea. They could not wait. The barbecue would have to wait. These wild, wild boys raced towards the sea throwing off their clothes as they went. Arthur, Edward, Tony, Francois, Harry and Phillippi followed. The splashing and shrieking did not stop until the smells of cooking beaconed. A pile of fluffy white towels was waiting for them. Wearing these huge white towels around their waists a Greek drama came to life as they lolled around on the grass drinking beer while the more grown up among them sipped wine on padded benches.

The very hungry boys fell on all the delicious food and for once Harry's manservant allowed himself a small smile.

Chapter 37
The Party

The development of the festival amazed everyone. It was all working so well. The villagers came up frequently to inspect, also the school mistress with all her children. The priest was ever present directing operations for the staging. He also found an electrician to do the lighting. The seedy electrician of the loose tongue was no more. Sophie and Ivy together helped the children with their English. And as the Priest predicted, Ivy's French improved. At the end of the day with everyone exhausted they trooped down to Harry's mansion to swim to eat and discuss progress. Edward and Tony had become very close. Hellen was extremely pleased to be back with her Aunt Sophie, and Sue spent a lot of time in the developing theatre and elsewhere with Francois.

Arthur seemed to be everyone's best friend.

Harry had become a great favourite in the village. He had been to see the Mayor, who agreed with him negotiating the acquisition of all the empty houses. The villagers were delighted that their village was coming to life again. Harry had everything in hand, it was almost finished and under budget. He felt it was time for a party. Most of the chairs were moved out of the salon. The lighting sorted and the kitchen expanded. Ladies from the village came up to help with the catering. Many delicious confections appeared as if by magic. And Harry, dear Harry, arrived with enough wine for the entire village.

The entire village came. The priest, resplendent in his white chasuble, said a long and formal blessing. Francois and his band played while Edward and Sue sang. How Edward loved to sing now, up in his mountain home. Everyone danced and sang, children ran around, and dogs joined in. Arthur was in his element, rushing from one group to another. The dancing continued well into the night, eventually friends from the village drifted back to their homes gently singing in the warm night air. Others crammed into their various pick-ups. Harry was to stay, as usual, on the daybed on the landing. He was not as tall as Francois, so found it quite comfortable.

All was quiet as the family sat on the terrace, reliving this incredible evening. But where was Arthur, and Scruffy? Ivy had seen them last sitting admiring his newly planted vineyard.

The moonlight, the ever-present smell of flowers and the occasional hoot of an owl followed Ivy as she picked her way under the olive trees. She could see Arthur and Scruffy asleep together in the distance, just as she had seen them many times before. They looked so peaceful, she did not want to wake them, but it was getting cooler.

This time she could not wake them. Arthur was not asleep. He lay there with Scruffy in his arms.

Ivy was not shocked, she had been expecting this. She sat down quietly beside him, taking his hand in hers. She had loved this man and was grateful for his peaceful end. She sat there for a long time, aware that his presence was still with her, a very precious time to be alone together. She finally became aware of the real chill in the night air. She knew she had to leave him and tell the others. She had to steel herself to leave.

She left slowly, glancing back only once. She was having difficulty breathing stumbling on the rough ground.

She entered the farmhouse.

All conversation ceased as they saw her. "Arthur has gone," she said quietly.

"He died with Scruffy in his arms – in his favourite place – overlooking his vineyard – I have said my goodbyes." She smiled a little secret smile and moved away.

The men left her with just Sophie. They had to bring Arthur back into the house. Sophie put her arms around her friend, gently rocking her.

The men carried Arthur back into the house, placed him on a long table in the centre of the salon and covered him with one of Ivy's best table clothes.

They left him having done their painful duty with Scruffy lying at his feet.

Chapter 38
Finale

It had been hot for the past few days and the land was like parchment, dry and pale as the continuous sun bleached all colour from the land.

As Ivy lay in her solitary bed, the huge wooden bed she loved she became aware that she felt empty, as empty as the bed. She was alone now, her other half gone. Silently she wept allowing the tears to flow.

In time she became aware of rain. She got out of bed looked through the window towards Arthur's vineyard. It would be grateful for the rain. She was grateful too. She moved over to the kitchen, her big friendly kitchen where her friends and family were gathered.

The priest arrived rather wet and breathless sheltering under a rather large black umbrella which gave him little shelter. He had arranged all that needed to be done in the village. Sitting around the kitchen table everyone reminisced about Arthur, the joy and laughter that he brought to people's lives. It was endless. It was decided that Edward would read the first lesson in French, followed by Tony reading in English. The priest would give a short talk in both French and English. The school mistress was already preparing the choir.

Phillippi's piano could be taken to the front of the church where he could play Fauvre's requiem, Arthur's favourite, at the beginning and the end. The Auberge had agreed to host a celebration for Arthur's life.

This interlude was rudely interrupted by the young campers noisily laughing and shouting about their experiences during the night. Their tents had come to pieces, they had spent hours trying to repair them – no success. They were exhausted soaking wet and had not had such fun in years.

Phillippi took charge. The young could camp in his new home in comparative comfort, He had lots of food. They all agreed this was an excellent idea. Sophie and Ivy accepted Harry's invitation to stay with him until the day of the funeral. The girls could come up to the farmhouse to help out, then move in with Francois. How that was going to work out was anybody's guess.

Harry drove the ladies down the mountainside as if they were glass. They did not speak. Ivy could not remember much of those few days except she had felt Arthur's constant presence around her and how much they laughed. *Odd,* she thought.

Back at the farm all was calm. Arthur's body had been taken down to the church to rest before the service. Ivy wanted to see him one last time, so with Sophie, Harry and Micky, she made her way through the the village; Scruffy not far behind.

Ivy was not prepared for the vision awaiting her. The entrance to the church was covered in a sweeping canopy of wild flowers. And as she walked through the massive doorway into the church itself, the scents of summer were overwhelming. The canopy of flowers continued all the way down to the altar where Arthur lay in a simple wicker cercueil.

Ivy walked alone down towards him.

She looked at him for a long while. She wanted to stay with him, but outside her friends were waiting. She had to leave.

"We must go to visit Phillippi," she said. Wanting to lift the gloom that had descended on them all. They agreed starting up the grassy slope towards Phillippi's house.

They could hear the noise before they got there. Through the gates, already repaired, they could see so much industry. All the boys were there with Phillippi and his new dog. The girls were arranging the house while Francois and his group were slapping white paint on the walls. They were all singing, mostly songs of freedom. It was completely uplifting.

The motor bikers were in the garden happily digging. They were really enjoying Grand pere in his new house.

Chapter 39
And the Sun Will Rise Again

The rain did not stop, a steady down pour covered the land, and even the trees seemed to be weeping at Arthur's passing. The sun did not shine that day. The chickens stayed in the barns and the dogs remained silent in the house. Even the birds did not sing.

There was no one to be seen in the village. The only sound was the tolling of bells. So many people were gathered outside the church, all quietly waiting in the rain.

Ivy arrived with Edward and Tony either side. She needed their support that day. Father Dominique, in splendid robes, was waiting for them at the door. He held Ivy's hand and smiled reassuringly.

Inside the congregation, packed the church. Men and women with babies, children sitting with the elderly, others sitting on the paving stones in the side aisles or leaning against walls. The sick had been brought in on stretchers or bath chairs. Dogs in possession of their owners huddled under seats.

Did they really know so many people?

Ivy could see the school mistress, the school children, their parents and grandparents. She saw the builders, the shop keepers and many others from the town below. Just about everybody they had met was there, all dressed in their best. Music filled the air. Phillippi was sitting at his piano playing. Ivy would not forget.

The choir with Francois and his group were magnificent. The readings were perfect. And from Father Dominique she felt a real love for his flock.

They had decided that Arthur should be buried on the farm at the far end of the vineyard.

After the service his coffin still bedecked with flowers was carried aloft by his sons and grandsons followed by Ivy Sophie and the girls. A minion truck was waiting festooned with wild flowers to take Arthur on his last journey.

Harry had somehow managed to acquire a splendid sort of bus for all the followers who were unable to walk. A multitude of people trudged up the track all unaware of the heavy rain pouring down upon them from above. They loved this man and wanted to be there at the end.

In the end is the beginning.